A
PALACE
IN
PARADISE

We gratefully acknowledge the support of the Canada Council for the Arts and the Ontario Arts Council for our publishing program. We also acknowledge the financial support of the Government of Canada through the Canada Book Fund.

A Palace in Paradise is a work of fiction. All the characters and situations portrayed in this book are fictitious and any resemblance to persons living or dead is purely coincidental.

Cover art: Heironymous Bosch, *Garden of Earthly Delights,* detail, ca. 1500, oil on oak panels, 220 cm × 389 cm, Museo del Prado, Madrid.

Cover design: Val Fullard

Library and Archives Canada Cataloguing in Publication

Title: A palace in paradise : a novel / Mehri Yalfani.
Names: Yalfānī, Mihrī, author.
Series: Inanna poetry & fiction series.
Description: Series statement: Inanna poetry & fiction series
Identifiers: Canadiana (print) 20190094451 | Canadiana (ebook) 2019009446X | ISBN 9781771336215 (softcover) | ISBN 9781771336222 (epub) | ISBN 9781771336239 (Kindle) | ISBN 9781771336246 (pdf)
Classification: LCC PS8597.A47 P53 2019 | DDC C813/.54—dc23

Printed and bound in Canada

MIX
Paper from
responsible sources
FSC® C004071

Inanna Publications and Education Inc.
210 Founders College, York University
4700 Keele Street, Toronto, Ontario, Canada M3J 1P3
Telephone: (416) 736-5356 Fax: (416) 736-5765
Email: inanna.publications@inanna.ca   Website: www.inanna.ca

A PALACE IN PARADISE

a novel

Mehri Yalfani

inanna poetry & fiction series

INANNA PUBLICATIONS AND EDUCATION INC.
TORONTO, CANADA

*To all those who believe
in freedom and human dignity.*

In return for deeds, the palace of paradise, they give.
    —Hafez, a classic Persian poet

CHAPTER 1

"As a tavah, *if you repent and cooperate with us, you'll have a palace in paradise. A palace in paradise, a palace in paradise...."*

THE SENTENCE RESONATES IN FERDOUS'S MIND but she tries to ignore it, focusing on reading her own handwriting. She wrote a goodbye letter to Ladan in case she died while donating her kidney to Frida. She wipes tears of joy and satisfaction from her face with the tips of her fingers; she's pleased with herself, as though she's accomplished something great. She feels nostalgia overcome her as she places the letter in the desk drawer. She found the desk a few years ago in front of a neighbouring house, and Ferdous smiles as she remembers how she and Nadereh dragged the old piece of furniture into the building from the sidewalk. They had struggled to fit it into the elevator, and later, through the apartment door, but all the while they had laughed and joked about their efforts.

Scattered haphazardly across her desk are her makeup, a pen and pencil, a notebook, and a discoloured white telephone. A dusty mirror, cracked corner to corner in a wooden frame, sits on the top shelf of the desk. She takes a tissue out of the box beside her. "That's much better," she mumbles to herself as she wipes the dust from the mirror. Her stomach aches with hunger. She goes to the kitchen to look into the refrigerator. She takes out a peach, which is partly rotten but still tastes good, then follows it with a gulp of water to wash down the lingering sweetness. She goes back into the bedroom and sits on the bed. A wave of hopelessness washes over her as she looks at the old curtains framing her grimy window. A ray of sunshine peeks into the room, leaving a spot of light on the carpet. Ferdous's eyes fix on the spot of sunlight. It's as if it's come to return hope and joy to her life, but Ferdous doesn't notice. Her thoughts are elsewhere. She needs courage. She is questioning the decision she made. "Everything is up to you," Nadereh had said. Yet, inside her stomach a hungry, hollow feeling persists. She thinks of the dinner she will have at Parvaneh's place; she always cooks a variety of rich, delicious dishes. Living alone, Ferdous rarely makes meals for herself. She only cooks Ladan's favourite dishes when her daughter visits. She ignores her hunger, but the question mark in her mind about her decision keeps growing larger and larger. Nadereh had planted the question: "Why should you give your kidney to Frida? You don't owe them anything."

She takes a few steps to the window, then returns and sits down on the edge of the bed. "I don't owe them anything, I don't, but Frida...."

Frida: Once a penniless dancer in a cheap café in Madrid. Frida....

Frida: Ghobad's wife. A wealthy young Iranian who lives in a mansion in Rosedale.

Frida has everything, everything, but she needs a new kidney. A new kidney that I'm going to give her. Am I? Should I? Maybe I shouldn't.

Unconsciously, she starts to hum a song. *"Tonight, I'm light-hearted, tonight I'm enchanted, once again tonight, I'm at the peak of the sky...."* The melody grows louder as it finds its way out of Ferdous's mouth, but it fades away when she gets up and walks over to her closet.

It's almost three o'clock, but Ferdous hasn't changed yet. She calls Parvaneh to confirm the evening's plan. She resolves to move forward with her decision. If she can ignore Nadereh, she will feel more determined and happy about her choice. However, Nadereh's words are like icy water splashing over her, drowning her joy and excitement about her "heroic decision," as Parvaneh describes it. Nadereh's words, repeating in her mind, bring her back to earth, helpless and now undecided. Exhaustion claims her body and her mind. Parvaneh's home is a long way away. *Shall I go or not?* It seems like it is a huge decision. *Why go? I can go to the hospital by myself. I don't need their help.*

Ferdous lives in North York, in the north part of Toronto, and Parvaneh's place is on the west side close to the Royal York subway station. To get there by public transit takes more than an hour and a half. She is supposed to be at Parvaneh's by four in the afternoon. She's already late, but she continues to hesitate.

Ferdous glances at her watch and approaches her closet. Since she came to Canada, she feels like she has grown taller. Her frame is slight, and her skinny body makes her look like a beanpole. She has no interest in food—she feels full after only a couple of bites.

Ferdous opens the door of her closet and stands there, staring at her clothes. She finally chooses a red shirt and a black skirt. She takes the skirt from its hanger and puts it on. It hangs from her body. She takes it off and throws it on the bed, then sits down on the edge. She remembers Ibrahim's words: "I didn't want to marry you. I did it because your father wanted it. I was twenty-two, and I was too young to get married. I felt sorry for you and your father. I wanted to get you away from that cesspool in Turkey. I didn't know." She reads the unspoken words in his eyes, "that you were a *tavab*."

Ferdous hasn't finished dressing when the telephone rings. It is Ladan. Dumbfounded, Ferdous asks, "What did you say? *Ghormesabzi?*"

"Alex asked me to make it for him," Ladan says. "He had it in an Iranian restaurant and now he's asking me to make it for him."

"Sweetheart," Ferdous says, "I'm getting dressed to go to Parvaneh's place. I'm late. It's not easy to make *ghormesabzi*. You need special ingredients, the right vegetables."

"What kind of vegetables?" Ladan asks.

Ferdous says impatiently, "You need *shanbelileh*...."

"Tell me what that is in English."

"I don't know the name in English. Now, sweetie, let me be. I have a million things to do. I'm going to Parvaneh's place, then tomorrow I have to go to the hospital...."

Ladan interrupts her. "What for? You're not really going to donate your kidney to Frida, are you?"

"Honestly, I want to see Frida. You know she has to stay in the hospital. Why don't you go to the Kabab House on Yonge Street for *ghormesabzi*. It's not that far from your place. If you go by streetcar you can be there in five minutes. Next week, I'll make roast vegetables for you or I'll even make *ghormesabzi* and bring it to you."

By the time she puts the receiver down, it's past three-thirty.

MRS. SARMADI, FERDOUS'S MOTHER, had come to visit when Ferdous was being treated at the psychiatric hospital on Queen Street West. Ibrahim had notified Mrs. Sarmadi and arranged for her visa.

"Ibrahim treated me very well," Ferdous told her repeatedly. "Yes, he wanted to rescue me from Turkey, from that chaotic situation. Do you think it was easy for such a young girl to be surrounded by all those hungry single men? The Iranians weren't the only ones. There were others, including Turks. All of them wanted to get you into their beds. It was a nightmare!"

A nightmare. A nightmare. A nightmare. The words filled Ferdous's mind.

Mrs. Sarmadi couldn't believe the state she'd found her daughter in, and Ferdous could sense it. Ferdous imagined her thinking, *How could this woman be Ferdous, my dearest child and precious jewel?* Before her eyes stood a simpleton with her mouth half open, her hair greying, her eyes cloudy in a deeply-lined face. She was stooped over like someone much older. Her daughter used to be tall and strong, her thick, long brown hair reaching to her shoulders. Her large bright eyes had never been sad, and a smile had never faded from her lips.

It took a while before Ferdous's mother pulled herself together and swallowed the lump in her throat. She hugged her daughter, stroking her hair, which felt like it hadn't been washed or brushed for days. Ferdous was so thin that Mrs. Sarmadi could feel her bones. She was distressed to see the grey in her daughter's hair. How many years had passed since they had seen one another! Ferdous pulled away from her mother and said, "Maman take me away from here. These people think I'm crazy. But I'm not. It just that I miss my daughter so much."

Ferdous asked about Ladan before she asked about her father. Mrs. Sarmadi still hadn't seen her ten-year-old granddaughter, who was living with Ibrahim's sister, so she lied: "Ladan is fine. She misses you too."

Ferdous had stared out of the window of the taxi and chewed on her nails all the way home. Every few minutes, she asked Nadereh, without looking at her, "Where are you taking me?"

Nadereh put her hand on Ferdous's arm and said calmly, "I'm taking you home. Your doctor released you so you could be with your mother."

When Ferdous and Nadereh entered the apartment, it was clear that Mrs. Sarmadi had swept and dusted. The windows were washed, and a Persian rug she had brought from Iran lay in front of the large sofa in the living room. There were new handmade cushion covers in various bright colours. The white lace curtains were washed and properly hung. The smell of steamed rice, saffron, and Iranian lamb stew, Ferdous's favourite food, permeated the apartment and seeped into the hallway. The worn and stained plastic tablecloth had been replaced with a new hand-printed one. A bowl of apples, pears, peaches, and grapes, and a dish of pistachios were on the table, along with a box of Iranian nougat.

Nadereh sent Ferdous in first. For a moment, Ferdous stood quietly inside the apartment door. Finally, she mumbled, "I can't believe I'm home. It reminds me of our home in Shemiran."

She removed her shoes and walked into the living room. Her mother hugged her and sat down beside her on the big sofa. Ferdous could see that her mother still couldn't believe this prematurely aged woman was her cherished and only daughter. Her mother could hardly keep her tears from showing and her pain from overwhelming her.

Nadereh sat at the dining room table, gazing at both mother and daughter. Mrs. Sarmadi shook her head, trying to keep her anguish at bay, and calmly announced, "I made some tea. Let me get it."

Nadereh got up so quickly that her purse fell off her lap. "I'll bring the tea," she said hastily. She went into the kitchen and returned with a tray carrying three glasses, the ones with the golden rims. Ferdous took one, raised it to her lips, and said, "I've always liked drinking tea out of this tiny glass." She looked at her mother and asked, "Do you remember, Maman?"

Mrs. Sarmadi said, "Of course, I remember. You had a special glass just for yourself. Do you remember how much you fought with your brother when he took your glass? You were...."

She didn't finish her words.

Ferdous nodded and said, "I lived like a princess in our house." Then she looked up at Nadereh, who had been watching them as they talked. "Yes, I was treated like a princess in my parents' home," she repeated, as if wanting to convince Nadereh. She also wanted to show her something about herself, something that no one might believe. "My mother always called me *shahzadeh khunum.*"

Mrs. Sarmadi smiled sadly and said, "You were a *shahzadeh khanum*." Then she corrected herself and continued, "You're still a *shahzadeh khunum*."

This time Ferdous laughed sardonically and said in English, "You're kidding me."

Mrs. Sarmadi looked at her, puzzled, and then at Nadereh, who translated. Mrs. Sarmadi turned to Ferdous and repeated firmly, "Yes, you are. I am not joking."

They drank their tea in silence, trying to hide their discomfort.

Ferdous looked at Nadereh and said, "Maman, if Nadereh hadn't been with me, I would have died. She helped me a lot. She is a very clever girl and she knows what's going on. There's Parvaneh, too. She's a social worker and her husband's a doctor. All of them are helping me. Don't think that just because we are not home in our own country that we don't care for one another. Ibrahim found this apartment for me. He has a friend who works at Toronto housing; he arranged it for me. The rent is low. Ibrahim helped this friend buy his house at a good price, and he helped me by getting this apartment. Did you know that Ibrahim is a real estate agent?"

LADAN HAD CALLED FROM THE AIRPORT to say she was coming home, so Ferdous went to the balcony to watch for her. When Ibrahim's grey Mercedes stopped in front of the building, Ibrahim and Ladan got out. He took a suitcase out of the trunk and led Ladan into the building. Ferdous opened the apartment door and stood in the hall, waiting for them to come out from the elevator. First a suitcase emerged, then Ladan. Ferdous hugged her tightly, then looked for Ibrahim, but he was already walking away. With a quick wave, he was gone. Helping Ladan with her suitcase, she wiped her tears behind Ladan's back. But Ladan felt her mother's tears on her cheek and asked, "Mommy, why are you crying?"

Ferdous continued to wipe away tears with the tips of her fingers and said, "Nothing. It doesn't matter. I am happy that..."

She followed little Ladan to the balcony and watched as Ibrahim got into the Mercedes and drove away. Ladan said, "If you only knew how nice Sussan is."

Back in the apartment, Ladan opened her suitcase. She took out a box of nougat and a package of pistachio nuts, saying, "Daddy bought these especially for you."

Ferdous looked at them indifferently and asked, "Did you go to see your grandparents? Did you see how big their house is?"

"Daddy didn't have time," Ladan answered. Then she took a small album from her purse and showed her mother Ibrahim and Sussan's wedding pictures.

IT WAS A SATURDAY AFTERNOON when Nadereh had called and invited Ferdous out for a walk. "Why are you staying home alone? Let's go down to the lake. Parvaneh told me that Ladan is with her father."

When Ferdous arrived at the lakefront, Nadereh was already there, sitting on a bench facing the lake.

The sky and the lake had formed a partnership in the dwindling summer afternoon. It was as if they wanted to say in their own way that this nice weather and this calm summer season wouldn't last much longer. In the distance, sailboats with white sails glided among the lumbering passenger ferries. Seagulls dotted the sky, their mournful cries adding to the sounds that disturbed the otherwise tranquil summer afternoon.

Together, they walked along the busy shoreline. People stood in line at a booth selling roasted corn. Nadereh bought two cobs, gave one to Ferdous, and bit into the other one as they continued to stroll along the boardwalk.

Ferdous said, "Wherever I go, whatever I do, I remember Ibrahim. Even though it's been more than fourteen years since we separated, I can't seem to forget him."

Nadereh stopped nibbling her corn and said, "Don't waste your time thinking about Ibrahim. He's certainly not thinking about you. Otherwise, he wouldn't have left after only a few short years of marriage and gone to Iran to marry a twenty-two-year-old girl."

"Nadereh, just think about what you're saying," Ferdous said, suddenly angry. "I told you a thousand times that Ibrahim didn't behave badly. Yes, he might not have been in love with me, but that wasn't his fault. Anyone in his place would have done the same thing. Look at me..."

She stopped talking abruptly, as if she couldn't find the words to explain how she felt.

"He still shouldn't have abandoned you," said Nadereh, more gently this time. "I think that if he hadn't left you, you wouldn't be depressed today."

Ferdous glared at Nedereh, holding the corn in her hand as though she were brandishing a weapon. When she finally spoke, there was a peculiar sadness in her voice, along with a trace of anger. "My depression has nothing to do with Ibrahim. He helped me get out of Turkey. Yes, my father gave us money. But if Ibrahim hadn't helped, I wouldn't have dared to come to Canada all by myself. I didn't know anything about Canada and you don't know anything about my life."

"You've left behind a harsh life. I know that. Anyone in your situation would be depressed. Ibrahim should have understood that. He knew that you had been a political prisoner, didn't he?"

Ferdous had only taken one bite from her corn. She stopped walking, and staring at Nadereh, tossed the corn angrily into the lake. Her voice was shrill. "Who told you I was a prisoner? For a period of time, I was in hiding. Then I fled across the border into Turkey. That's when my father came to Turkey with Ibrahim."

Nadereh placed her hand on Ferdous's arm and said, "Yes, I know. You've told me the story several times. I haven't told anyone that you were a prisoner. I didn't really know anything about it until Parvaneh told me. It's none of my business."

FERDOUS BANISHES THE DISTURBING MEMORIES from her

head, dresses hastily, and stands in front of the desk, looking into the mirror. The crack that cuts the mirror in half cuts Ferdous in half too. When she brought the table home, she had planned to change the mirror, but she hasn't gotten to it yet. Her complexion is sallow, and there are dark shadows around her eyes. She powders her face, dusts some rouge onto her cheeks, and green eye shadow on her eyelids, then adds some red lipstick. She smiles at the reflection of herself in the mirror and mumbles aloud, "That's much better."

She remembers Frida's words. "Have you really decided to give me your kidney? That's so wonderful. I'll be in your debt as long as I live." When she said this, Ferdous felt a sense of pride and happiness she had never experienced before.

Now, standing in front of the mirror, she tries to revive those feelings. When she is ready to leave, she glances at herself one more time in the mirror in the hallway and smiles. By the time she steps into the street and looks at her watch, it is almost four. She has to run to catch the bus and makes it in the nick of time, her heart beating rapidly. She smiles, satisfied. "I made it," she whispers to herself.

Sitting in the bus and staring blankly out the window, she thinks again of Nadereh's earlier admonitions. "They should be looking after *you*. Why do you want to give something to them? You don't owe them anything."

Does she? She doesn't know. Yes, she does. No, she doesn't, yes, she does, no, she doesn't.

If Ghobad and Frida abandon her, Anis and her family will do the same, as they have done for many years. When she was in the psychiatric hospital, they didn't even come to visit her. Ibrahim had his own reasons—he wasn't her husband anymore. But Anis was a close relative, her daughter's aunt. She didn't even bring Ladan to see her mother in the hospital. If only for Ladan's sake, Anis should have at least asked about her, Ferdous thought.

Ferdous doesn't say any of this to Nadereh. She doesn't

want to portray her ex-husband's family as evil; she doesn't
want to think of them that way. However, Nadereh can read
her mind. She is the only person who has stayed by her. "You
can behave the same way," Nadereh says. "If they don't care
about you, you don't have to care about them. You don't
really need them."

Everyone who knew that Anis had raised Ladan said, "What
a good sister-in-law! Imagine, raising your ex-sister-in-law's
child. It's really too much to ask."

By adding the words "too much," they were insinuating that
helping Ferdous out wasn't worth the effort.

Ferdous doesn't tell Nadereh that she needs Ibrahim's family.
Even if she doesn't need their money and even if she doesn't
take anything from them, she still needs them. They are like
large shade trees under which she is able to rest. She doesn't
need to pick their fruit; she needs their attention and their
acceptance. Anis, her husband, Ghobad, and his family are
respected members of the Iranian community. To be respected and have a good reputation is very important to Ferdous,
Nadereh, on the other hand, doesn't care.

"They accept you grudgingly," Nadereh tells Ferdous. "Do
they ever invite you to their home when they invite 'respected
people,' as you call them? They maintain their relationship
with you just to boast about how kind they are to you. They're
using you."

Ferdous secretly agrees with Nadereh, but she doesn't say
anything. She listens, but continues to defend her in-laws.
"I owe Gobad and Frida something. Ghobad gave me a job.
Frida took Ladan into her home. My poor little Ladan had
no family in this country. Her mother is mentally ill, confined
to a psychiatric hospital off and on, and her father doesn't
want her. He gave her away to his sister, Anis. God bless her
husband, who was like a father to my baby, and Anis, who
took my daughter to Ghobad and Frida's home. Ladan became
friends with Ghobad's children. My child...."

Ferdous stops. She swallows the lump in her throat and wipes tears from her eyes. After a bitter silence she continues, "You don't know how painful it is to lose everything. You haven't experienced this. Remember, your father was a factory worker and you were an orphan child, raised by your sister's family. But before I left Tehran, I was living in my father's house. Even when I was in hiding, I lived in my father's house. My father made a tiny passage behind the shelves in the library and I hid in there. Whenever I heard the doorbell I would hide in that tiny space. The revolutionary guards came to search our place once. They were looking for my brother, Keyvan, who was with me, but they couldn't find us. It didn't cross their mind to look behind the bookcases. Yes, I believed in the Quran. I read Dr. Shariati's books. I learned the verses of the Quran by heart. But I was nobody, not important. My father wouldn't let me join political groups, but while I was in school, he had no control. The students forced you to mix with them and become politically active. I don't know who reported me, but when the revolutionary guards came looking for me, they were really after Keyvan. He was the one who was politically active. But, after everything, they couldn't arrest me, nor could they arrest Keyvan." She stared at something far away, and her words trailed off. She doesn't want Nadereh to know the truth, about her brother, about herself. She is silent.

"Don't talk about it anymore," Nadereh tells her. "Think only about yourself. No one cares about you. You need to take care of yourself."

Nadereh's remarks—*No one cares about you, no one cares about you, no one. No one, no one*—become a drumbeat in Ferdous's mind.

CHAPTER 2

WHEN PARVANEH OPENS HER EYES, the morning light is filtering through the white blinds, giving the bedroom a delicate cast. She turns to Mahan, whose back is to her; a muted buzzing sound issues from his half-opened lips. Automatically, she stretches her arm to embrace her husband, but then she remembers that Ferdous, Nadereh, and Goodarz are coming to visit that afternoon. She has to get up early and prepare. She is filled with despair and mild anger; she's annoyed with herself and the visitors who have already spoiled her Saturday. Mahasti has ballet class today, and it's Parvaneh's turn to take her. She forces herself to get out of bed. Mahan wakes up and rolls over. In a sleepy voice, he asks, "Where are you going this early in the morning?"

Smiling, Parvaneh puts her hand on Mahan's shoulder and says, "I have lots of things to do. You know that."

Mahan opens his eyes. "What? It's Saturday. Have you forgotten?"

"No, I haven't," says Parvaneh. "You have to be at the hospital too. I have to take Mahasti to dance class and then go shopping. Remember, Ferdous, Nadereh, and Goodarz are coming over. Frida is going to be hospitalized today, and then tomorrow..."

"But I'm not going to the hospital today," Mahan says. "Kim swapped his shift with me. He's going on vacation next week. So I can take Mahasti to her dance class." He closes his eyes again. "Don't worry about it," says Parvaneh. "It's my turn. I'll take her myself. But I have some other things you can do."

Mahan opens his eyes. "What? To tell you the truth, I don't know why they have to come over here today. If Ferdous is going to donate her kidney tomorrow, she shouldn't be eating anything tonight anyway. That's a major surgery. It's not a joke."

"Frida isn't having the surgery tomorrow," says Parvaneh. "They've postponed it till the day after tomorrow. I'm supposed to make a light dinner and serve it around four or five. It is better for Ferdous not to be left by herself. I asked Nadereh to come over, too. She's her only friend, and Goodarz might come with Nadereh."

Completely awake now, Mahan asks, "Nadereh? What's Nadereh got to do with this business? It's Ferdous who is going to donate her kidney. Why did you invite Nadereh?"

"I told you," Parvaneh says, "I thought it wouldn't do any harm if Nadereh accompanied her to the hospital. Besides, she needs someone to look after her. I can't do that all by myself."

Mahan says, "You said that Nadereh was against Ferdous donating her kidney. You said..."

Parvaneh kisses Mahan's cheek and gets out of bed. She draws the curtains and lets the morning sunlight flow across the carpet and the bed. "Yes, she's against it," she says. "But for Ferdous, it's already a done deal."

The sky is clear except for a few bits of cloud, and the bright fall sunshine lights up the courtyard and the lawn. Mahan rests his head on his arm and watches Parvaneh move around the bedroom.

"Thank God," Parvaneh says. "Hurricane Juan blew over. It really didn't do as much damage as they expected it to. It probably lost its strength."

As she turns to smile at Mahan, he asks, "Who's Goodarz, anyway? What's his relationship with Nadereh?"

"How should I know?" Parvaneh replies. "She says he's her roommate. A homeless man she found in the street." Parvaneh stands by the door and adds, "This is Nadereh we're talking about, remember? Don't you know her?"

Mahan says, "You're only making things difficult for yourself."

"It's my job," Parvaneh sighs. "I have no choice."

Brushing her teeth, Parvaneh acknowledges that Mahan might be right. She is simply making trouble for herself. But, she thinks, "It's what I do. I have no choice. If I had a choice I wouldn't do it, but with Nadereh it's different."

Standing under the shower, she lets the water run over her head and drain off her body—it's as if she wants to wash away any troublesome thoughts from her consciousness. She is a social worker. It's her job to get involved in other people's problems. Applying solutions from the books she has read or from her own life experiences, she provides gentle suggestions while allowing the person seeking a solution to take ownership of their problems and their ultimate resolution. The comfort and pleasure she gains from helping others are far greater than any payment she could ever earn.

When she steps out of the tub, her image appears ghostly in the steam-covered mirror. She brushes her hair back. Her face has a healthy flush, and her big brown eyes sparkle. Her prominent cheekbones have taken on a glow, and her smooth skin belies her age, making her appear much younger than she really is. "If only I were a little taller," she thinks, looking at herself. This has been her only complaint about her appearance since her teenage years.

Parvaneh isn't as tall as her brother and sisters. "You made me from the leftovers of all your other children," she used to say to her mother. "When you conceived me, it wasn't out of love but rather dismay. Maybe you just didn't have the energy for me; that's why I am so short. You produced your best for your other three children—they are all tall—but when it was my turn you didn't have anything left."

Barely tall enough to reach Mahan's shoulders, she has to

wear high heels when they're out together. Because she lacks height, she also needs to be careful about how much she eats. She says even a tiny bit of food causes her to gain a few kilos. Her prominent breasts are another problem; they make her look heavier than she is. But her curly hair, short and dyed a light brown, is always lustrous and silky to the touch.

Parvaneh pulls on her robe and goes back to the bedroom. Mahan has gotten up. She opens her closet and searches through her clothing, finally settling upon a pair of white pants and a colourful shirt. She dresses and afterwward applies some moisturizing cream to her face. The delicate scent of the cream fills her nostrils. Then she goes to Mahasti's room. Quietly opening the door, she enters the room where her daughter is still sleeping, her long dark hair spread across the pillow. Parvaneh sits on the edge of her bed and silently gazes at her. Then she takes the girl's hand in hers and leans down, kissing the little girl's fingers one by one. Mahasti moves a little but doesn't wake up. Parvaneh plants a loud kiss on her forehead. Awakened, Mahasti half rises and hugs her mother, wrapping her arms around her neck.

"Did you take a bath?" she mutters sleepily.

"Yes, my love, and you should..."

"I have to take a bath too?" Mahasti frowns.

"You know that today you have to go to dance class. I'll take you to visit your Aunt Farnaz after."

"With you and Daddy?"

"No, only you. We're having guests. I told you that last night."

"But I want you and Daddy to be with me, too."

Parvaneh is still holding her daughter's hand in hers. She kisses Mahasti's palm and then the back of her hand, as if performing a ritual, speaking in between kisses.

"No, sweetheart, no, my love, we can't come with you. Daddy and I have work to do. We are having people over this afternoon. But we may come later."

"Why can't I stay with you?"

"If you get up quickly and get ready for your class, I'll tell you why on the way. Now, be a good girl...."

Her last kiss proclaims all her unbridled love for her baby. Parvaneh rises from the bed and lifts Mahasti from under the covers, but Mahasti lets herself go and falls back onto the bed again. Parvaneh puts her hand on the girl's shoulder and says, "Come on, my dear, get up. You have to go to class."

Her mother's words, although loving, carry a sense of urgency, so Mahasti grudgingly climbs out of bed. While Parvaneh makes the bed, Mahasti changes into the outfit that her mother laid out for her.

In the kitchen, Mahan has made the toast and set out butter, cheese, and jam on the table. At Mahasti's place is a bowl for cornflakes and a carton of milk.

The early fall sun casts a delicate light through the window. The lawns are green and petunias and nasturtiums are still blooming in the flowerbeds. Some of the sunflower stalks are bent because of yesterday's storm, but the morning sun promises to give the flowers a new lease on life. The tall cedar in the front yard resembles a happy young woman with no fear of the coming winter or the loss of any leaves. It casts its long shadow down the wall.

As Mahasti enters the kitchen, Mahan is placing the toasted bread in the basket. Mahasti runs to her father, and he turns to greet her, taking her into his arms and showering her with kisses. Father and daughter remain in this position for a moment. When Parvaneh enters the kitchen, she laughs and says, "That's enough hugs and kisses for now. Let's eat our breakfast and be on our way. We don't have much time."

Mahan promptly deposits Mahasti on her chair, then pours some cereal into her bowl and adds milk. When breakfast is over and Parvaneh is ready to leave, Mahan asks, "Do I have anything else to do besides making the Olivieh salad?"

While searching through her purse for the car keys, Parvaneh looks at Mahan and replies, "Cook some pasta, please. I'll buy some cold cuts at the deli on my way home." She takes out the car keys and continues, "You'll have to tidy up the house a bit, too. Don't forget."

Mahan takes the last sip of his coffee, and nods, "That's my weekly chore, anyway."

Mahasti runs to kiss her father goodbye. Mahan hugs her and plants a kiss on the top of the head as she snuggles into his neck.

"Come on, sweetheart, that's enough for now," Parvaneh says.

Mother and daughter leave the house together. Parvaneh takes her place behind the wheel and Mahasti scrambles into the back seat. Parvaneh starts the car and begins backing down the driveway while Mahan waves goodbye to them from the doorway. Parvaneh waves back and Mahasti blows a kiss to her father with her hand. As the car starts down the street, rounds the turn, and is lost behind the trees, Parvaneh thinks about the busy day she'll have. She tries to calm herself down, but there's a flame of anger in her. She tries to ignore it.

IT WAS TUESDAY AFTERNOON. Parvaneh had just finished her telephone conversation with Ferdous when the phone rang again. The rings seemed louder and sharper that time, like a person screaming hysterically in the midst of a nervous break-down. It was as though an invisible person were shouting, "I know you're there, so answer the phone." But Parvaneh didn't want to answer the phone. There wasn't that much time left until the end of the workday, and she had to rush to pick Mahasti up from her school. Still, thinking that it might be Ludmina, her supervisor, she reached over and grudgingly picked up the receiver. "Maybe she has something urgent to tell me," she thought, putting the receiver hesitantly to her ear. But it was Nadereh's voice at the other end of the line.

Nadereh was agitated and got directly to the point. She was always the same—when she had something important to say, she got right down to it. She didn't even ask how Parvaneh was feeling. "You've got to talk to Ferdous. You have to stop her from doing this."

When she realized what Nadereh was talking about, Parvaneh tried to collect herself and said, "Ferdous has made her decision. Next week…"

Nadereh interrupted her angrily, "I know, I talked to her last night. She's crazy. That stupid woman doesn't know what she's doing. You and Mahan should stop her. Mahan should explain to her…"

She looked at her watch and wanted to say, *I have to go. It's late. Mahasti is waiting for me.* But there still was half an hour left in her day.

"Nadereh, please do not meddle in Ferdous's business. She is not a child.…"

Nadereh's voice became louder and hoarse. Parvaneh held the receiver away from her ear and cursed Nadereh under her breath. Her earlier telephone conversation with Ferdous had made her happy. Ferdous was proud of her intention to donate her kidney to Frida. "Poor Frida, she'll die with her failed kidney," Ferdous had said. "Poor Samanta and Sasha—if their mother dies…"

"You're doing a good thing," Parvaneh had told her.

"Everyone says so, everyone except Nadereh."

"It's none of her business. You need to make your own decision."

"I've made my decision."

Nadereh's voice brought her back. "You should talk to Ferdous yourself," Parvaneh said, trying to keep the anger out of her voice.

She had been doodling meaningless lines on a pink piece of paper, one square inside another. She wanted to say, *talk about what?* But she held her tongue. She knew that Nadereh would not let her go until Nadareh felt she'd convinced Parvaneh. In order to cut her off, Parvaneh finally concedes. "Very well, come to my place on Saturday, you and Ferdous. You can explain everything to her. However, I think if you listen to her, you'll change your mind."

"Which Saturday?" Nadereh asked. "This coming Saturday? You said that Frida is supposed to be hospitalized this week. Won't Saturday be too late?"

Parvaneh couldn't control her anger anymore. "Nadereh, do not meddle in Ferdous's affairs," she said firmly.

Nadereh asked crossly, "Can you tell me why? When she had all her problems before, I was the only one who looked after her, and now I have to sit back and do nothing. Am I missing something?"

Parvaneh looked at her watch: it was twenty minutes to five. She said, "It's important that you hold off and stop meddling," she answers. "This is something Ferdous has to do for herself."

Nadereh asked hesitantly, "Is there something I should know that you haven't told me? I…"

Parvaneh interrupted her, "I haven't told you this—I'm sure no one has—but Ferdous was a traitor, a *tavab*."

Impatiently, Nadereh said, "You've already told me that," Nadareh replies impatiently. "You also told me that you want nothing to do with anyone's past. And I shouldn't have anything to do with her past, either. As you said, we aren't the *anker* and *monker* for all people, are we?"

Parvaneh waited for a moment for her anger to dissipate. Her forehead felt hot. The paper on her desk was covered with doodles. She said, "Yes, I did say that. But I think with this decision, Ferdous believes she can atone for her past…"

Nadereh interrupted her again.."I don't understand it."

"It's better to stay out of it," Parvaneh said, "and let her make her own decision." Again she looked at her watch and said, "I really have to go and pick Mahasti up. You know that poor Frida is counting on Ferdous's decision. Everything has been arranged."

"I don't understand it," Nadereh repeated.

"I'm sorry," Parvaneh said coldly. "I have to go. Come over

to my place on Saturday. On Saturday we'll talk about it. I'll tell Ferdous to come over, too."

She hung up and was immediately sorry she had made the suggestion. As she put the receiver down, she asked herself, *Why my place? What does any of this have to do with me?*

MAHAN HAD PUT MAHASTI TO BED and had come back to the kitchen. He sat the table, picked up the newspaper, and paged through it at random. Parvaneh was standing by the kitchen counter drying the dishes, something she rarely did. She usually left the dishes to dry in the rack but she had wanted to prolong her chores. She wasn't sure Mahan was pleased about her news.

"What do you think?" Parvaneh asked. "Who is right? Nadereh or Ferdous?"

"What're you talking about?" he muttered, without lifting his head from the paper.

"I'm talking about Ferdous donating her kidney to Frida. I told you Nadereh is against it."

"Nadereh?" asked Mahan absent-mindedly.

Parvaneh faced Mahan and said, "You're not saying anything. What's your opinion?

"Why is my opinion so important? This is none of my business." He put the newspaper down on the rack and left the kitchen.

PARVANEH HAD MET MAHAN for the first time at her friend's wedding. They were both still in Iran. Nastaran had said, "He's a friend of Hamed. His name is Mahan. He went to medical school with Hamed, and now he works in a public hospital. He's a good catch. His mother is dead and his father is a lawyer or a judge, but he's remarried and has his own family. To be honest, he'd be a perfect husband. Don't let him get away."

Parvaneh had laughed, then hugged and kissed Nastaran and congratulated her on her marriage to Hamed. But Nastaran was insistent, and had whispered in her ear, "There he is, the one I talked to you about a few days ago—your ideal future husband. Go and get to know him. Hurry up before you miss your chance."

"How?" Parvaneh asked timidly. "I'm embarrassed."

"You feel shy?" Nastaran laughed loudly. "Since when are you shy? Okay, wait a minute, I'll introduce you."

She held Parvaneh's hand and led her to the corner where Mahan was standing. He was talking to a tall, slender girl, who was wearing a long black dress with a colourful scarf covering her bare shoulders. Her long reddish-black hair reached her waist.

"Mahan, this is Parvaneh Khanum. She's the one I talked about a few nights ago."

Before she had a chance to say anything else, Hamed appeared at her side and pulled Nastaran away to introduce her to some other friends.

Parvaneh was left standing with Mahan and the tall, long-haired girl.

"Nastaran forgot to introduce me to you," the girl said. "I am Sima. I've come from Canada to visit my parents and attend this wedding. I am surprised that men and women here now mix freely and without women having to wear their veils. It's just like being in Canada."

"Only in the privacy of a house," Parvaneh said.

"And not without fear and anxiety," Mahan added.

"Also with someone to bribe the guards," Parvaneh chortled.

"Oh, I see," Sima said and nodded. "I've learned a lot in these past two weeks."

Sima reached over to get a piece of pastry from a dish on the table nearby, and Parvaneh moved out of her way. She found herself closer to Mahan but she turned toward Sima and asked, "How's life in Canada? I know you don't have to wear a veil, but what about the other things? One of my sisters has been there for four years now. She's very happy. My other sister wants to immigrate as well, but her husband is not willing to go."

Sima popped a rice cookie into her mouth and said, "No pastry can compete with ours. I've gained two kilos since I got here."

Then wiping the crumbs from her mouth with the back of her hand, she continued, "Excuse me, you asked about Canada? Well, it depends on the situation. If you have money, all doors are open to you, just like anywhere else in the world. But if you are forced to go as a refugee claimant and work in the black market and study, well that's another story..."

She paused, then added, "But no matter what, you can make your way if you're willing to work hard."

"I think it would be very hard to start a new life in a foreign land," Mahan said. "Living at home still has its benefits."

Sima was still eyeing the dish of pastries. "As my father says, you needn't die in misery just because you were born here," she replied.

"If I am not mistaken, that quote is from Saadi." Mahan said.

Sima laughed loudly and said, "But I heard it first from my father." She took a cherry from a large fruit bowl, held it up to Parvaneh, and said, "Can you tell me which poet wrote a poem about cherries?"

Parvaneh stared at Sima absent-mindedly.

"Forugh Farkhzad," Mahan said, and looked at Parvaneh, waiting for her to confirm it. But it seemed that Parvaneh hadn't heard Sima's question or Mahan's answer; she looked lost in thought. After a while, she said, "Sima might be right. When you can't live freely at home, you're better off leaving."

The room was filled with loud music. "I've missed Iranian dancing," Sima said. She gazed longingly at the young girls and boys dancing at the far end of the hall, where the lights were dimmed. She smiled at Mahan and Parvaneh, and asked, "Do you dance?" When Mahan and Parvaneh did not respond, she turned and made her way over to the other side of the room.

Mahan and Parvaneh stared at each other for a moment. They both blushed. Mahan took his eyes off Parvaneh and glanced at the dancers, then looked back at Parvaneh and said, "Do you dance?"

Parvaneh shook her head. "What about you?" she asked.

"No, not for a long time."

After a while he continued. "When I was a child, whenever there was a gathering at our place, there was music and dancing, too. My father played tar, my brother was learning santour, and sometimes my mother accompanied them on the drum. We had..." his voice trailed off.

They sat side by side, silently watching the dancers. Parvaneh turned to look at Mahan, who stared back at her. Changing the subject, he asked, "Do you want to go to Canada too? These days, everyone you talk to is either back from Canada or is going to immigrate there. Canada has become the promised land for many young people and families."

Parvaneh said, "Everyone has his or her own reason for immigrating. But I've got a job here. And I can't leave my mother—she'd be all alone."

"It's good to have a sense of belonging," Mahan said. "I think in a foreign country one loses the feeling of connection."

If someone is with his or her family, there's no reason to lose a sense of belonging," Parvaneh remarked pragmatically. "My sister immigrated with her husband and her two sons. At the beginning it was a little hard for them, but now they seem to be very happy over there. They don't complain."

TWO WEEKS LATER, THEY WERE IN A RESTAURANT, having dinner, on Takhte Jamishid Street, which had been changed to Taleghani Street after the revolution. The waiter placed a plate of bread and butter on the table and took their orders. After he had gone, Parvaneh started the conversation by commenting, "The revolution changed the name of this street but not this restaurant."

Mahan was quiet for a while. A look of pain flashed across his face, then he sighed and said, "But the revolution took my brother." Parvaneh, shocked, did not know how to respond. Soon he continued, "Then my mother had a stroke and became paralyzed. She died six months later, and our family was torn apart. My mother was too young to die. She wasn't fifty yet. My brother's death was a severe blow."

He stopped talking and stared out the darkened window. Night had completely spread over the city. The waiter came back with two dishes and two soft drinks.

They busied themselves mixing butter into their rice and adding sumac to their kabobs. After they had each eaten a few morsels, Mahan asked in low voice, "Have you heard of Khavaran?"

"Khavaran? No, I haven't. Is it a prison?"

"No, it's a mass grave. My brother is buried there without a gravestone or a marker of any kind. He was in prison for more than six years. He was supposed to be released. He had completed his sentence, and every week my parents travelled to Tehran to bring him back, but one day..."

He stopped suddenly.

Parvaneh was speechless; as if she was listening to a horror story. Her heart pounded in her chest, and her hands gripped her fork and spoon.

Mahan continued, "My brother was in his third year of medical school when he was arrested. It was so hard for my parents to accept his death. I still can't believe it. My mother was such a lively person; my father was, too. They'd married out of love for one another. But then when my mother died and when my father remarried, I couldn't bear it. He might have been right to remarry. He had to live. He couldn't mourn the rest of his life for his son and his wife. Life goes on, no matter what happens. I was angry with my father then, but now I think he did the right thing."

Mahan smiled, even though tears were welling up in his eyes. He turned away and wiped them from his cheeks. When Parvaneh put her hand on his, he looked at her and smiled sadly. "It didn't only happen to our family. It happened to many families. A friend who lives in Germany told me that more than four thousand were killed. In the few months after the war ended, it was a real massacre. But, as you can see, life is still going on. It seems this is part of our history, always sacrifice and martyrdom."

He breathed deeply and continued, "As Sohrab Sepehri put it, '*A storm arrived and wiped out my footprints.*' He smiled at Parvaneh, but tears filled his eyes again, even as he tried to hold them back.

Parvaneh squeezed Mahan's hand again and said, "Nothing could have been done. We who are left behind should be able to live again. We should cherish life."

Mahan smiled cautiously. "Do you think so?" he asked. "Was it really impossible to do anything?" He ate a spoonful of his food reluctantly, as if he were being forced.

Parvaneh tucked an unruly lock of her hair back under her colourful scarf. She didn't answer Mahan. She was uncomfortable talking about politics when she had only known Mahan for two weeks. Could she trust him?

Parvaneh swallowed and said, "The revolution didn't tear my family apart, even though it had its effects. My father became depressed and then died of a stroke after he was forced to retire. He was a colonel in the Shah's army. After my father's death, my brother Sohrab took his wife and daughter and moved to America. His daughter has a learning disability, and he believed there would be more opportunities for her in the U.S. Then it was my sister Farnaz's turn. When her sons were old enough, they would have had to go to the front line to fight Iraq. So instead they went to Canada. First they applied for immigrant status, but they were denied, so they chose to be refugee claimants and were accepted with the help of a lawyer. Now it's my second sister Soraya's turn. Her daughter hasn't been accepted into a university, and her son isn't doing well in school; she's afraid he'll become mixed up with drugs and

maybe become an addict. So, she's also decided to immigrate
to Canada."

"Everyone has their own reasons for pulling up their roots,"
Mahan said. "It's not an easy task. Even if you haven't been
forced to..."

"What about you?" Parvaneh asked.

"No, not me. I don't think I'll be able to abandon my home.
My mother and my young brother are buried here. How can
I leave?"

Parvaneh looked at him in silence. Mahan was playing with
his leftover food. "If my father hadn't married again, I'd return
to Saary and work there; the place where I was born and grew
up is very special to me. Every neighbourhood in the city has
a special memory for me. They're mostly sweet memories—all
my childhood memories. Well, Tehran isn't a bad place, either.
Its crowded streets and traffic jams bother me, but I've been
living here for ten years now."

"People make memories everywhere," Parvaneh said. "When
Sohrab was still in Iran he kept saying he missed America.
He talked mostly to Catherine, his wife, about their shared
memories. They talked about the small town they had lived
in after they had married and its beautiful park, full of people
having picnics in the summer."

"He might go back to America now because of Catherine?"

"Yes, I think so. It is mostly because of Catherine, not their
daughter, Ela. Catherine is American, so Sohrab considered
himself partly an American too, because of his marriage to her.
Haven't you ever heard the joke? When a man is asked where
he comes from, he says, 'I haven't married yet.'"

Mahan smiled, pushing his plate a little further away. He
blushed shyly and asked, "Where are you from?"

Parvaneh looked at Mahan, her cheeks also turning red. She
said, "I was born in Tehran, but both my parents were from
Shiraz."

"Can I say that I'm from—?"

Parvaneh didn't let him finish. She said, "You've already said that you were born in Saary and grew up there."

Mahan put his hand on Parvaneh's.

She said, "I've already told you, I am from Tehran." The colour spread from her face to her neck.

Mahan squeezed her hand and said, "And you're a social worker. I knew that, and now can I say I'm from Tehran, too?"

Parvaneh blushed more deeply and felt hot with joy and shyness. She said, "You should talk to my mother first."

"You mean you can't make a decision?"

Parvaneh smiled, her heart beating faster in her chest, and said, "I've made my decision. That is only a formality."

THERE WERE ABOUT TEN OR TWELVE social workers in the workshop. During the break, Nadereh, who knew only Parvaneh, told her, "I don't think most of these social workers are honest with people. After they leave their office they forget about people's misery."

"You're very idealistic," Parvaneh said. "No one can carry other people's burdens. It's impossible."

Nadereh nibbled her muffin, sipped her coffee, and said, "So, maybe it's better to be in another profession. I think a social worker is like a doctor who has a pill for everything."

"I do my best, but..."

"When I first arrived here, what you did for me was special, and I'll never forget it. Not everyone gets that chance."

MOTHER AND FARNAZ HAD COME TO VISIT Parvaneh. It was a few months after Nadereh had arrived in Canada. Nadareh was still living in a women's shelter, but she visited Parvaneh often and sometimes stayed overnight. She wore a mustard-coloured shirt of Parvaneh's that was too big for her tiny figure, and her old, discoloured jeans were worn out at the knees. It was Saturday, and Mahan was at the hospital.

Parvaneh introduced Nadereh to her mother and Farnaz.

Nadereh had Mahasti on her knee and was playing with her fingers, singing children's songs to her. A few minutes later, Mahasti took Nadereh's hand and said, "Auntie Nadereh, let's go to my room. I want to show you my white bear."

Nadereh took Mahasti by the hand and they ambled out of the kitchen together.

"Who is this little waif?" Farnaz asked. "Your home is turning into a homeless shelter."

"What beautiful eyes she has!" Mother said. "How innocent she seems!"

"She's only twenty-two," Parvaneh said. "She's suffered a lot. Many of her family members were killed in the war. Her husband, I guess, was a political activist. He was killed too."

Farnaz peeled an apple, cut it into pieces, and offered it to her mother and Parvaneh. She said, "All of them were political activists and had painful stories—just look at us or Soraya and Siamak. If we hadn't been involved in politics, they wouldn't have accepted us." She smiled contemptuously.

"We have to believe whatever they say," Parvaneh said. "Even if we don't, we shouldn't show it."

"I know," Farnaz said. "Just like our lawyer. But tell me, why do you bring the homeless into your home?"

Parvaneh took an orange from the fruit bowl and started to peel it. "Her parents and her sister were killed in the war," she said. "And her husband was killed in the street fighting. She was left abandoned in the street with nowhere to stay. She turned to a smuggler to get out of the country."

Farnaz shook her head scornfully. "Be careful, my dear. She might bring diseases into your household."

Mother looked at Farnaz, frowning. "The king has pardoned the victim, but his minister hasn't. Mahan is the one who should be against her. He's not, so why should you be?"

"I'm saying this because of Mahan," Farnaz said. "I'm afraid Parvaneh is going to make trouble for herself."

"You think everyone is like your husband, always chasing

after women?" Mother said, pursing her lips in annoyance.

Farnaz leaned back in her chair. "Since when has my husband been chasing other women? I'm just worried about Parvaneh."

Parvaneh wanted to add, *Mahan isn't a lecherous man, either,* but when she looked up and saw Nadereh and Mahasti standing by the kitchen door, she stopped talking.

"IT'S AN EASY VOLUNTEER JOB," Parvaneh had said some weeks later. "You don't need to know English very well, and you don't need any Canadian experience. I'll entrust Ferdous to you. And you'll get your TTC pass for free. You told me you want to get some more experience in social work. This is a chance to get some hands-on training. After you pass your English test you can enroll in college and continue your education."

"Who's Ferdous anyway?" Nadereh asked.

"She is a devastated Iranian woman," Parvaneh said. As she searched through the scattered papers on her desk, she continued. "Her husband betrayed her and took her child away from her. The poor woman ended up in an institution. She has nobody here. Once in a while I go and visit her. They say she was a political prisoner for a while, but she denies it. Some people say she was a *tavab*. You know what a *tavab* is? A collaborator! They say she betrayed her own brother and her close friends, and today she feels guilty and miserable. But we shouldn't judge her because of her past. We need to help her. Help her if you can, Nadareh. She is so unhappy."

PARVANEH RUNS INTO LOBLAWS to do her shopping. The line to pay is long, and it's close to one o'clock in the afternoon when she finally gets to put her shopping in the car. She is supposed to be home before three and she still has to pick Mahasti up from school. Nervously, she thinks, if something happens, it will be her fault. She wishes she hadn't invited Nadereh to her home. What does Nadereh want from her, anyway? Why won't she leave her alone? Farnaz was right when she said, "Don't let Nadereh get to you. You're giving her too much credit for helping Ferdous."

It is her mother who thinks a lot of Nadereh. "It's my own fault. I shouldn't have let her get so close to me, Parvaneh says to herself." Then she justifies it to herself, "She isn't really such a bad girl."

When she goes to pick Mahasti up, she can't stay more than a few minutes to talk to her teacher. Hurriedly, she gets Mahasti into the car and drives to Richmond Hill. She parks in front of Farnaz's house and rings the bell. Hassan opens the door wearing gardening gloves; his pants are worn out at the knees. Mahasti is sitting in the car and doesn't want to get out. On the way, she told her mother that she doesn't like to stay with Auntie Farnaz because they don't have any children to play with. Parvaneh replied she has no other choice because the people coming to the house might be speaking about things that she shouldn't hear. Parvaneh has put a few computer games and a drawing book in Mahasti's knapsack so she can amuse herself.

Parvaneh greets Hassan with a hug and asks, "Isn't Farnaz home?"

"Yes, she is, but she's with a customer."

Farnaz has made wedding gowns ever since she arrived in Canada and bought the Richmond Hill house. She keeps a few wedding dresses at home for people to rent. She joins them at the front door and shoos them inside. "Why are you standing here? Why don't you come in?"

Parvaneh kisses Farnaz and says, "It's late." She looks at her watch and runs toward the car. Taking Mahasti's hand, she pulls her out and carries her knapsack to the house. "I have to go. I'll come get her this evening."

Farnaz takes Mahasti by the hand and says, "Don't bother. Behnood and Suzanne are coming over. Mahasti is going to be busy."

Mahasti jumps up and down and says, "Really? Will Sara be here too?"

"Yes, sweetheart. She's walking now. You should see how cute she is! She's learned a few Farsi words like *maman, baba, awb*."

Parvaneh says, "I've got to go. Sorry for bothering you."

"Don't worry about it. When Mahasti wants to go home, I'll call you. If your guests leave early, come for dinner. Hassan is going to barbecue."

As Parvaneh drives away, Farnaz and Mahasti stand by the door and wave goodbye to her. She suddenly feels happy to have immigrated to Canada, even though she had to argue with Mahan for months to convince him. When they arrived, it took more than few years until he passed his exam and was able to practise as a physician. She had her sisters here to rely on.

IN MEHRABAD AIRPORT, after Parvaneh's mother had entered the departure lounge, Parvaneh wiped the tears from her eyes and said to Mahan, "There's no one left. They're all gone."

Tears rolled down her face again when they exited the terminal. Though it was late autumn, some trees still had leaves. A chilly wind was blowing, and the air had a hint of rain to go with the familiar smell of smog. Gloomy clouds were taking over the sky. Together, they walked arm in arm towards Parvaneh's Renault. She handed the keys to Mahan and said, "I don't feel like driving." She wiped her tears with a crumpled tissue.

As they drove off, Mahan said, "This separation has started to become a regular part of our lives. If it's not because of death, accident, or execution, then it's these immigrations, wanted or unwanted. You'll just have to get used to it, like me."

Parvaneh said, "My father's death was easier for me to bear than my mother's leaving."

Mahan turned and looked at her. "I can't believe it," he said. "Death is very hard to bear. It's worse because it's irreversible, but with immigration, there's always the chance of returning. And also you can go and—"

"Yes, death is irreversible, but when my father died, I had other people around me, and I was younger, too. Now, I'm very lonely."

Mahan was driving very slowly. "Your mother won't stay away forever," he said.

"I think she's gone forever. Farnaz says she's going to apply for her immigrant status—the facilities for old people are much better over there. Here there would be no one to look after her except me."

CHAPTER 3

WHEN PARVANEH'S CAR DISAPPEARS around the curve in the street, Mahan goes back into the house. He's sitting at the kitchen table reading the paper when the telephone rings.

"Good morning. How are you today? Is Parvaneh there?"

Immersed in the article he is reading, it takes him a moment to come back to the present. There is a strange tone to Nadereh's voice; he isn't quite sure what it is. Is she going to scold him or appeal to him for support? He hesitates before answering.

"Hello! No, Parvaneh isn't here. She took Mahasti to her dance class, and then she's going shopping. She'll be back around two o'clock. Did you want to speak to her?"

"No, I didn't necessarily want to talk to her," Nadereh says. "I wondered if Ferdous is going through with her decision?"

Mahan looks at the kitchen clock over the door; it shows ten-forty. Before he can answer, Nadereh continues. "Is there anything that I can help you with? I'm free today."

Mahan feels his heart speed up slightly. "No, not really," he says. "Parvaneh's got it all arranged." He wants to say, "You can come by if you want," but he manages to bite back the words.

"Well, okay then," Nadereh says, sounding disappointed. "I just wanted…"

"Is there anything else?"

"No."

"Bye then. See you later." Feeling hot and sweaty, he puts

the receiver down before Nadereh says goodbye then quickly picks it up again, but the line is dead.

He gathers the newspaper from the table and puts it back in the basket. He has completely forgotten what he just read.

PARVANEH CALLED HIM FROM HER OFFICE and said, "I'm going to be a little late today. Can you pick up Mahasti from daycare?"

He had just gotten home and was filling the kettle with water for tea when Parvaneh arrived, accompanied by a slight young woman with curly black hair tied neatly at the back of her head. She had big, dark brown eyes. A strange feeling came over Mahan as he watched the woman sitting at the kitchen table, looking around. She was like an innocent child entering a strange new environment.

During the two hours the girl was with them, he racked his brain trying to figure out whether he had met her before. Nadereh hardly spoke more than a few words to him. When she was not playing with Mahasti, she was quiet and looked around with a strange sadness on her face.

Parvaneh settled the girl in her mother's room after dinner, then came into their bedroom. Mahan still felt he knew the girl from somewhere, but he couldn't place exactly where. And if he had met her, was it in Iran or here? Or maybe he knew someone who looked like her? Because of the nature of his job, he was always meeting people, but this girl was different. She conjured up a strangely familiar feeling—not pathos or pity, but a familiar curiosity.

Parvaneh slipped into the bed beside Mahan and said, "That poor girl has lived a horrible life. If I told you only part of it, you wouldn't believe it. I don't know how much of it is true, but if one tenth is, it's still terrible. She lives in a shelter, and they sent her to me today to see if I can find an English class for her or help her get a volunteer job. She looks smart, but she is also very innocent and childlike. I couldn't send her back to the shelter, so I hope you don't mind that I brought her home for one night. She looked so lonely and so lost."

MAHAN MAKES THE POTATO SALAD and puts it in the fridge. Then he adds the pasta to a pot of boiling water. While the pasta cooks, he vaccums the living room. Sunshine streams through the window and onto the sofa. He reminds himself to tell Parvaneh they have to move the sofa so that the sun won't discolour it. Outside the window, he can see the street is silent and peaceful: a car passes occasionally, and the maple trees lining the street are still green in the warm fall sunshine. Mahan is left with the sound of the vacuum and his thoughts. He thinks about his telephone conversation with Nadereh. He feels himself being overtaken by a vague anxiety, the same forbidden attraction he experiences whenever she is around, or when he and Parvaneh visit her.

MAHAN WAS SITTING AT THE KITCHEN TABLE, Reading the morning paper, when Nadereh entered the kitchen, wearing a nightgown that she had borrowed from Parvaneh. Her curly hair framed her face, making her appear mysterious and at-tractive. Her dark brown eyes set off her baby face; her tiny perfect teeth, small pointed nose, and high cheekbones made her look like a Barbie doll. The gauzy nightgown revealed her small but statuesque figure. After three months of visiting Parvaneh and Mahan, Nadareh no longer felt awkward or shy in front of Mahan, but she was surprised to find him still at home. Pouring a cup of tea and sitting at the table, she asked why he hadn't gone to work. Mahan replied that he was on the afternoon shift.

Suddenly Mahan's face brightened with amazement. He had just remembered where he had seen her before. "You..." he started, then stopped suddenly, fixing his eyes squarely on her face.

Nadereh looked at him, puzzled.

"Your eyes," he stammered. "Your eyes remind me of someone. I remember a woman..."

Nadereh interrupted him. "If it's a love story, it can't be me."

Folding the newspaper and setting it aside, Mahan said, "No,
no, not a love story, but a very sad memory. When I was a
resident in a hospital in the south of Tehran, a young woman
came in one day holding a dead child in her arms...."

The smile vanished from Nadereh's face, and her eyes opened
wider. "And what does this have to do with me?"

Mahan's voice took on a clinical tone. "That woman's eyes
were exactly like yours. I can see the same defencelessness in
them. I have been wondering where I've seen you before, and
now I remember."

"What happened to that woman? Was her child really dead?
Or did the child die in the hospital?"

Mahan frowned. He looked like a child whose favourite toy
had been taken from him. He said, "I told you her child was
dead before she brought him to us, or he died in the hospital
before I saw him. His body was still warm, but he had stopped
breathing and had no pulse. I don't know how long it had
been, maybe a few minutes, but nothing could be done. The
child was dead, but the mother..."

His voice was full of genuine sorrow. A silence fell between
them. Shakily, he continued, "Her eyes.... There was a pain in
her eyes that was impossible to see without feeling her sorrow.
For a doctor, death is an everyday occurrence. For me, the living
are more important. I've seen lots of death, many people who've
lost their loved ones. But this, this was different. Her black
eyes—they weren't completely black, they were like yours, but
there was only desperation and sadness in them. I wanted to
hug her. I thought in that moment that she needed sympathy,
a warm hug. I didn't think I could console her with words. I
didn't even know her. It was the first time I had seen her, but
I still wanted to hug her. But when I moved toward her, she
stepped back. She had such horror in her eyes that I was scared,

too. I pulled away. Believe me, there were no words for her. There was a lump in my throat and I wanted to cry. I asked myself, why didn't she let me hug her or soothe her? I didn't want to hurt her. You may not believe it, but I still think the same thing. Why do people build walls around themselves?"

Nadereh was quiet for a while, her eyes fixed on the ground, contemplating Mahan's words. When she finally looked up at him, there were tears in her eyes.

"Were you...?"

Nadereh didn't let him finish his question. She pursed her lips, then vehemently stated, "No. That was not me." Then, she got up and quickly left the kitchen.

Was Nadereh the same young woman from the hospital in Tehran? Mahan was convinced she was, even though she denied it. If she was, it would remain their secret; he would never tell Parvaneh.

MAHAN HEARS THE TELEPHONE over the sound of the vacuum, but he doesn't care. Let it ring. Standing by the window, he looks out into the front yard, absorbed by the sparrows hopping around searching for seeds. Then he remembers the pasta and rushes to the kitchen. The water in the pot has evaporated, but the pasta isn't burned. He empties the pasta into a strainer and runs it under cold water.

He returns to the living room to finish vacuuming. The sound of vacuum cleaner wraps him in solitude, and more memories come to the surface. He thinks about when he was a high school student in Saary and his brother a medical student living in Tehran.

It was a Friday morning and Mahan was still in bed. The sky was cloudy and he had slept in. He could hear his mother talking to Nezhat over the sound of vacuum cleaner in the living room. Nezhat came every Friday to help his mother clean the house. It was huge, with its spacious rooms and vast courtyard that looked like an orchard. Mother couldn't manage it by herself. Outside his window, the leaves of the orange tree whispered softly in the breeze. The leaves were a soft green, and their gentle fluttering was calm and soothing. His mother used to say that green was the colour of spring and revival, and that it represented hope.

Fridays were Mahan's favourite day because he didn't have to wake up early and go to school. He didn't enjoy school the way he had before the revolution. In those days, life had been carefree and learning was easy. Now most of the senior students were absorbed in politics; differing factions continuously debated various political viewpoints. More often than not, this perpetual debate led to frustrations that too often boiled over into physical confrontations. Mahan was not a senior and tried to avoid aligning himself with any group. He longed for the childhood that had been cut short by the political events, and he still enjoyed his mother's hugs and morning kisses. During breakfast his mother showered attention on him before helping him dress to attend school with his older brother, Massood.

Ever since Massood had left for medical school in Tehran, Mahan had been lonely. No one could fill the void his older brother had left in his life. The thought that he too must leave his parents' comfortable and familiar house depressed him. The colleges and universities were closed; Mahan didn't talk openly about it, but he wished they would never open again. His parents were worried about Massood, who didn't know what to do in Tehran while the universities were shut.

From his bed, Mahan had been watching the branches of the orange tree swaying with the breeze when the first raindrops began to splash against the window. He was absorbed by the different sounds the rain made as it fell among the leaves and against the window. Suddenly the sound of the vacuum stopped, and he heard someone outside the door.

He listened closely as the outer door opened and closed, and then a man's voice began to speak. At first he supposed it might be his father, but he knew his father went to poetry and Sufism sessions with his friends every Friday.

Suddenly his bedroom door swung open and Massood strode in. Tossing his knapsack into a corner, he boomed a greeting to Mahan and promptly sat down on the bed. "Why are you still in bed? Are you sick?"

Mahan smiled, embarrassed, but didn't say anything.

"Don't you know what time it is?" Massood asked reproachfully. Without waiting for the answer, he continued, "It's a quarter to twelve! Don't you have any homework?"

Mahan got out of his bed. His heart was full of joy.

"LET'S TAKE THIS NEW PATH," Massood had said. "It's beautiful." Mahan peered at the narrow path winding among the trees, the leaves glistening in the sunshine. The path promised to lead off into a mysterious land, but, farther down, they could see that the tree branches grew closer together and blocked their way.

"Are you sure we won't get lost?" Mahan asked.

Massood laughed loudly and patted Mahan's back saying, "Lost? We aren't five-year-old children."

As they started down the trail bathed in golden sunshine, Mahan asked nervously, "Do you know the way? Have you come through here before?"

Massood had his hand on Mahan's shoulder. It was as if he wanted to keep him from turning back. As they headed into the forest, he parted the overhead branches and ducked his head, and said, "We have to try a way we haven't tried yet. I'm sure we won't get lost. These trees are our friends. They won't let us get lost."

TAKING A BREAK, MAHAN SITS ON THE SOFA and looks pensively out at the plane tree; its leaves are still green. A single tear slides down his face. In the street, a car drives by. Mahan checks his watch, remembers Parvaneh, then gets up and continues to vacuum. Again, the noise of the vacuum fills the house as he busies himself to finish the cleaning in preparation for the evening's guests.

THEY PASSED BY THE BOOKSTORES on Revolution Street in front of Tehran University. Mahan stopped in front of a one with medical texts in the window.

"Why did you choose to study medicine?" Parvaneh asked. "It doesn't suit your character. You're the sensitive type, more interested in poetry and literature." It was a few months after they had met. Their wedding date was set.

"I'm interested in books and…"

"And what?" Parvaneh asked.

"I chose to be a doctor because of Massood," Mahan said. "I wanted to follow his path, but he was somebody special. And I'm not like him."

"How so?"

"It's hard to explain."

HE GOES TO THE KITCHEN and dumps the pasta into a ceramic bowl, adds some mayonnaise, vinegar and olive oil, and then puts it in the fridge. He says to himself, if it needs something more, Parvaneh will take care of it. He takes a bottle of water from the fridge and drinks from it. The clock shows two forty-eight. There is not too much left to do, he thinks to himself. He is glad that Nadereh hasn't shown up early.

He takes a cigarette from the fridge and lights it, opens the door to the backyard, and blows the smoke out. Briefly, he worries about Parvaneh catching him, but then he dismisses his concern.

MAHAN TOOK THE CHILD FROM HIS MOTHER. He looked into the brown-black eyes staring at him from out of her pale face. "I'm sorry," he said mechanically, "it's too late."

"Is he dead?" the woman asked.

Mahan nodded. The child was on the examination table. The woman placed her hand on the child's head and stared at Mahan. It seemed as though she wanted to say: *Do something for him, make him alive again.* Mahan shook his head sadly and looked at the woman. He struggled to control himself and said, "I'll call for a doctor to write a death certificate." And he hurried from the room.

HE PUTS OUT HIS CIGARETTE, then takes the vacuum to Mahasti's room on the second floor, and plugs it in. The sound engulfs him like a thick fog.

THEY'D GONE CAMPING AS A GROUP: Mahan and Parvaneh, her two sisters and their families, and Nadereh and Ferdous. They'd erected their tents close together. At night they made a fire and sat around it, eating snacks, telling jokes, and talking about their sweet and bitter memories.

On the second day, they all went hiking in the forest despite the cloudy weather. Mahasti was mostly carried on Mahan's shoulders. On the way back, Parvaneh took Mahasti's hand and hurried ahead with her sisters so she would have time to give Mahasti a bath at the campsite. Mahan followed along with their children, Hassan and Siamak. Nadereh and Ferdous were lagging behind, so they decided to wait until they caught up. Nadereh was limping—her shoes were hurting her feet—and Mahan suggested she sit on a fallen tree trunk and rest for a moment.

"Take your socks off, too," Mahan said, "so I can see what's wrong."

"It's not important, Mr. Doctor."

Nadereh's sarcastic retort hurt Mahan, even though he wasn't really sure how he felt about her. He wanted to be around her, but at the same time he wanted to get away from her. He was attracted to her, but she made him very uncomfortable.

Mahan knelt down in front of Nadereh. Suddenly, she

reached out and took Mahan's hand and said, "These hands don't look like a doctor's hands to me, they're too fragile and slender. They're probably good for writing poetry. Why did you become a doctor, anyway?"

Ignoring her question, he pulled his hand back and examined her feet.

"It's not serious..."

His voice trailed off. Sitting beside Nadereh in the silence of the forest, he suddenly found himself unable to say a word.

Silently they sat in the lush green of the glade. The clouds had begun to break up and sunshine was beginning to penetrate through to the forest floor. At first, Nadereh was staring off into space, but she suddenly turned to Mahan and returned his stare. He couldn't take his eyes off her.

"Did I tell you that I was born in Ahwaz? I lived there until I was ten or eleven. The summers there are like a hell," Nadereh said.

"Have you ever been to Khuzestan?" Without waiting for his reply, she continued. "If you have, it was probably during Nowruz in Abadan for a holiday. Lots of people came to enjoy the warm weather and the shopping in Abadan and Ahwaz."

He said nothing. He was thinking of the woman with a dead baby. There was something in Nadereh that stirred him. As if she could read his mind, Nadereh said, "If I am not mistaken, you're thinking of that woman again."

He hadn't realized how long he had been staring at her without speaking. Then they kissed.

When he regained his composure, Nadereh had disappeared into the trees. In that moment, he had lost consciousness of his surroundings. He could still feel her lips, and her perfume lingered, leaving him weak and slightly intoxicated.

He avoided looking at Nadereh for the rest of that day. At night in his tent, he tried to remember how it had happened. The only thing he recalled was Nadereh's eyes; she had told him she had inherited them from her grandmother, a gypsy who had travelled through the south of Iran on foot until she was forced to stay at home by her husband. That evening, he was tormented by and ashamed of what had happened. He knew he couldn't talk about it with Parvaneh; he was overcome by guilt, but the forbidden pleasure he felt was hard to ignore. Sleep wouldn't come.

At dawn, he was still awake. He lay on his back staring at the ceiling of the tent. As the birds began their chorus, Parvaneh stirred and woke up. He turned his back to her, pretending to be asleep. She called quietly to him and put her hand on his shoulder as she did every day, and they listened to the birds' songs in silence. Later that day, he made an excuse to return to the city alone. He let Parvaneh and Mahasti come back with her sisters. For days, he agonized over the incident, wondering whether to talk to Parvaneh about what had happened between Nadereh and himself. He eventually chose to say nothing. Nadereh stayed away for a while, and the episode gradually faded from his mind, but sometimes it still disturbed him. *What if Parvaneh ever found out?*

WHEN MAHAN IS FINISHED VACUUMING Mahasti's room, he moves on to their bedroom. He doesn't hear the sound of the front door opening, so he's surprised to find Parvaneh putting away the groceries when he returns to the kitchen.

"When did you come back?"

"You were busy vacuuming. I didn't want to disturb you."

"What did you do with Mahasti?"

"I left her at Farnaz's. Farnaz asked us to come over this evening. Hassan is going to barbecue."

As they talk, Parvaneh washes the fruit, leaving it to dry in the strainer.,

There are beads of sweat on Mahan's forehead and his face is red.

"Do you feel hot?"

"Your vacuum sounds like a jet engine."

Sitting down at the table Parvaneh says, "To tell you the truth, I wish this whole thing wasn't happening today. I'd rather have this day to ourselves. We rarely get any time to ourselves without Mahasti."

The sudden ringing of the telephone startles her. Mahan says, "If it isn't Mahasti, it's the telephone." From Parvaneh's greeting, he can tell it is Ferdous. Mahan wishes she wasn't coming.

Setting the phone down Parvaneh says, "Ferdous wanted to know if it was still okay to come today."

"You told her it was."

"I couldn't tell her that it wasn't. We'd already planned it."

Mahan is about to mention Nadereh's phone call, but he hesitates. Then, reluctantly he says, "When you were out, Nadereh called. She wanted to know if there was anything she could do to help."

"Did you tell her to come earlier?" Parvaneh asks.

"No, I didn't. We don't have that much to do. They're not supposed to stay for dinner."

"No, not for dinner, just *Olivieh* salad and some pasta. Only for…"

"For having enough energy to be able to talk. You're such a patient person."

"What could I do? I had to. Someone has to take Ferdous to the hospital. Who else is there except Nadereh? And now she's going to try to change Ferdous's mind. Why? I'll never know. She thinks she's helping Ferdous, but she's just getting in the way. Do you remember that refugee claimant boy who was supposed to be deported? She wanted to marry him to prevent his deportation. Then they found out that his father was a billionaire and there were millions of dollars in his account. He could have bought the whole immigration offices. And then there's this Goodarz—he's an addict and a not well. She lets him stay at her place. She says it's temporary, but he's been living there for a few months now. It's none of my business if there is something going on between them or not. If they sleep together or not, it's their own business. To tell you the truth I don't really know Nadereh very well, either. At times, she seems very complicated. Sometimes she risks everything. Really, I wish she wasn't coming over tonight. I just didn't want Ferdous to go to the hospital by herself, but I couldn't go with her. What would I have done with Mahasti?"

Mahan gets up and says, "I'm going to take a quick shower. Vacuuming always makes me sweat." Leaving the kitchen, he says, "Don't be so hard on yourself. Try not to say anything that might hurt someone's feelings. Don't take one side over the other. Just try to be impartial."

"Is that even possible? What if they ask my opinion?"

"If they ask your opinion, tell them that they know best what they want to do."

"Really? I wouldn't have thought that. Have you forgotten that I'm a social worker? I have to give some advice, the same way you hand out prescriptions."

Mahan stands at the door for a few minutes and says, "Nevertheless, don't say anything that would bother anyone, and don't be so worried."

CHAPTER 4

NADEREH IS KILLING TIME, enjoying the nice weather and watching people in front of the Eaton Centre. There is a man sitting on a stool beside her, and she watches him sketch a portrait of a girl. She looks about eight or nine, and she smiles shyly for the man and her mother, a tiny woman with long, wavy black hair.

It is shortly after three in the afternoon, and the area is crowded with people. Nadereh hasn't been home since ten in the morning, when she left with Goodarz to go to the reference library on Yonge Street. After spending an hour reading the newspapers, she decided to take a walk, telling Goodarz that she would call Parvaneh to see if she needs any help. Goodarz lifted his head from his book and said, "You go, I'll come later." When Mahan told her that Parvaneh isn't home, she changed her mind about stopping by early.

Now she's wandering about, wiling away the afternoon until it's time to head over. She reaches the lake. She likes to spend time here, but today she's restless. Lately, whenever she is supposed to go to Parvaneh's home, she becomes unreasonably anxious. When she talked to Goodarz about it, he said, "It is a symptom of disease."

"What kind of disease? Typhoid? Asphyxia?"

Goodarz didn't respond.

It's three o'clock in the afternoon by the time she gets back to the Eaton Centre. Many people are walking around, mostly young boys and girls, some in groups, some in pairs, some by themselves, a mixture of races and nationalities. Some of the young people sport the latest piercings: lips, nostrils, eyebrows, tongues. There are young girls who even wear a ring in their exposed navels. Clothing ranges from leather dresses to blue jeans, the latest styles in many colours, often with metallic ornamentation, all accompanied by dramatic hair styles in a rainbow of hues.

Nadereh loves the Eaton Centre area—wandering around, taking in all the chaos around her usually puts her in a good mood. Sometimes there is a musician playing the guitar and singing. Sometimes two, three, or even more play drums, and people stay to watch and listen to the frantic music, tossing coins into the musicians' hats. When the weather is nice, there are a few artists selling portraits of celebrities, particularly Elvis Presley and Michael Jackson.

Today, though, Nadereh isn't in the mood to walk around, and the afternoon seems to go on forever. Edgy and anxious, she decides to go back to the library and then on to Parvaneh's with Goodarz. *But what if Goodarz isn't there or doesn't want to go?* That morning he'd told her, "I might go. I'm kind of interested in seeing what you've got in mind for the poor woman. It's none of my business, but well...."

Feeling hungry, she buys a hot dog and a soft drink. She finds an empty bench, sits and eats her hot dog, and then heads to the Dundas subway station instead of the library.

NADEREH SAT OPPOSITE PARVANEH at her desk. Behind the desk, Parvaneh had an air of authority, which subdued Nadereh.

"You have to have a strong case to be accepted," Parvaneh said. "You'd better think about it before talking to a lawyer so you can give them something impressive."

"I'll tell you my story, and if you think that my reasons aren't good enough, maybe you can add something that will get their attention."

Parvaneh left the office and came back with two big mugs of coffee. Closing the office door, she put one on her desk and one in front of Nadereh,

"My grandmother was a beautiful gypsy woman. I never met her, but my mother said her beauty was incredible. My grandfather was a smuggler, trafficking in the Persian Gulf. They say that after he married my grandmother, he left a girl in her belly and then disappeared. The story goes that he went to Bahrain or Kuwait to smuggle contraband, but drowned at sea. After my grandmother raised her daughter and found her a husband, she became a gypsy again. I don't know whether she married again or not. My mother didn't talk about her very much. I heard these things from other people. My father was a labourer in the Ahwaz steel plant. We had a tiny house—I don't know if my father bought it or if it belonged to the company. There were five of us, all girls. My father was killed by a missile at the beginning of the Iran-Iraq war when he was helping behind the front lines. Then everybody told us we'd better leave Ahwaz since it was being shelled every day by artillery.

"My mother's answer always was, 'I'm not going anywhere. How can I move somewhere else with four girls.' She said, 'I'm going to stay here until my children and I are all killed.'

"It happened just as she predicted. I was ten then. Not even two months after my father's death, my mother and my younger sister, who was six years old, were killed by the shelling. They went to buy bread and never came back. I was left with my two sisters. Mahboobeh my eldest sister was married before the war and had left for Andimeshk. When the war started she moved to Tehran with her husband and her child and stayed there. Of the three of us left, Fatima was two years older than I was and Razieh was four years older. Razieh was tall and sturdy like my mother. She looked like an eighteen-year-old, but she was younger.

"We had nobody in Ahwaz. My father had come from a

tribe in the central area of Iran. I never could figure out which one. One day, two months after my mother's death, Razieh came home with a soldier. His name was Morad. She said she was going to marry him. She got permission from one of my father's co-workers, who was a close friend of my father's and considered himself our guardian. After their marriage, Morad lived with us. Fatima and I were happy that we had a man watching over us. We had my father's salary, so we weren't in need. Two weeks after my sister's marriage, Morad was sent back to the front lines. He said he would take my sister to to stay with his parents, who lived in a village between Shiraz and Behbehan, leaving Fatima and me all alone. When we asked what would happen to us, he said that we could go stay with our eldest sister in Tehran, but we hadn't heard from her since she had moved away, and we didn't even know where she lived.

"So instead, my sister and I went with Morad and Razieh. We lived with Morad's parents for three years until he finished his military service. In the meantime, he came home several times on holidays, and he and Razieh had two children. Morad's mother taught my sister and me to weave carpets, and we didn't go to school anymore. Fatima was in grade seven and I was in grade four when we had to quit school. Morad received my father's pension each month and told us he was using it for our expenses. Fatima and I sat behind a loom weaving carpets all day long and produced one or two rugs every month.

"One day when I woke up, Fatima wasn't sleeping beside me like she always did. I thought she must have gone to the washroom. Then I found out that she had left. She had taken her clothing and all her belongings. Morad said, 'She has gone of her own free will, let her go.' Razieh was worried that she would go back to Ahwaz and claim our father's pension, and that there would be no more left for me, but Morad assured her that Fatima was still a minor and therefore wouldn't be able to transfer the pension.

"I never saw Fatima again," Nadereh said bitterly."

"What happened then?" Parvaneh asked.

"Time passed, and I became older and wiser. I told my sister that I wanted to go back to school. In the village where we lived there was a mixed school for boys and girls. My sister took me to the school, but they wouldn't accept me. I was thirteen by then, and the principal said I was too old to be in an elementary school.

"Morad told me to wait a little longer, that he was planning to move the family to Shiraz. He was a teacher, and the following year he got a job. I moved to Shiraz with my sister and her family. Morad's mother didn't come with us. She said her home was in the village and she didn't want to give up her land, but she was sad to lose me when we moved. She had never had a daughter. She never treated me badly, but she never let me waste my time for a single minute. I either sat at the loom weaving rugs or did the housework. Her fingers were disfigured because she was always weaving rugs, and she had constant pain in her knees and her back.

"In Shiraz, I registered in night school and wrote the final exam to pass grade five. I still hadn't finished grade seven when I met Ehsan, who attended the night school too. It was the wintertime when we met. The days were short and it got dark early. He walked me home to my sister's house after classes. We became friends and I told him my life story. His own story was more or less like mine, and we sympathized with each other. Originally, he had lived in Dezfoul, a city that was attacked by the Iraqis regularly during the war. He had been at school when a bomb fell on his house and killed his parents. His brother, who belonged to a political group, had also been killed in a street fight.

"Eventually, I fell in love with Ehsan. I wasn't happy in my sister's house. Like her mother-in-law, my sister wanted me to work for her. She, too, expected me to weave rugs. All day long I was either behind the loom, washing her children's clothes, or doing the dishes. Morad treated me the same way.

Both of them thought of me as their maid. I worked for them to earn my living, despite the fact that Morad still received my father's pension.

"I told Ehsan, 'Let's run away and go to Tehran.' Ehsan said, 'You don't even know me yet.'

"I said, 'My sister didn't know Morad, either, and now they are married and have two children. My other sister ran away from home and she probably has a husband and children by now too.'

"'You're only fourteen. You are still a child,' Ehsan said.

'Not fourteen,' I said. 'I'm almost fifteen. And Islamic law states that a girl can marry at nine years of age.'

"We planned everything in secret. On the last day of school, we got on a bus, and the next day around noon we were in Tehran. I had never been to Tehran before. Ehsan told me we were going to stay with one of his father's friends for a few days and then find a place of our own. It was an old house with a small pond in the middle of the courtyard and tall sturdy trees full of leaves. Although Ehsan had told me the house belonged to his father's friend, I never figured out who the owner of the house was. When we arrived, there was a middle-aged couple with no children, and at first I thought they were the owners. Then there were other people who came and stayed there for one or two nights at a time; they sometimes left late at night. After a couple of weeks, the couple left too, and they never came back. They didn't say a thing when they were leaving. Then Ehsan told me we had to leave too. He said that, in order to rent a room, we should pretend we were brother and sister coming from the war zone. No one believed us though—we didn't even look alike. I'm dark, as you can see, but Ehsan had a pale complexion and light hair with light brown eyes.

"We spent about a week sleeping under bridges or in deserted alleys. Then we went into the suburbs and found an empty hut that we made into a home for ourselves. I didn't know where Ehsan got his money from. When I asked him once, he said that I would be better off not knowing about it. After a few weeks of living in our little house, I realized that he belonged to a dissident group. He gave me some pamphlets to read and explained his ideology to me—he was fighting for the working class. A few weeks later we became intimate and began to sleep together. I told him that we should be officially married. I didn't want to do anything against my religion, and I thought that if we became husband and wife we wouldn't have committed any sins. Ehsan said he had no birth certificate and his real name had to be kept secret; otherwise, he could be identified and he would be arrested, tortured, and executed. After he told me the truth about himself, he said that I would be better off not getting involved with him. Because I was still a minor, he told me, I could go back to school, finish my education, and get my high school diploma. But I insisted on staying with him. I had no other place to go, and, in my eyes, we were almost husband and wife.

"The next afternoon, we decided to seek out one of his distant relatives. They had heard what had happened to Ehsan's parents and his brother. They felt sorry for him and welcomed him. When Ehsan said he wanted to marry me, they understood the position we were in and arranged for us to be married. The next night, Ehsan's great uncle, who was a clergyman, performed a simple ceremony for us, and we became husband and wife. We stayed with them for three days and then returned to our hut in the south of Tehran. Ehsan didn't work, so I decided to look for work myself.

"We stayed in that hut for about three months, and then cold weather forced us to move into a room in a house in a suburb of Tehran; it was almost a village, I suppose. All the people coming and going were politically active.

"We had been married for five or six months when I realized that I was pregnant. Around this time, Ehsan disappeared. Twenty-four hours after he left, one of the men in the village told me that he had been recognized and could possibly have been arrested. Now I understood what being 'recognized' meant. He told me that I had better find a place to hide or go back to live with my family. He said that if they caught me, they would force me to confess everything I knew. I didn't have anywhere to hide, and they came for me that very night. It was in prison that I found out Ehsan had been killed in the street, fighting."

It was now past two o'clock and Parvaneh was very hungry. She had been concentrating on recording Nadereh's story, but finally she asked her to stop for a break.

Taking a big sandwich from her purse, she gave half to Nadereh, then left the room with their two empty mugs and came back with two cups of tea. She devoured her sandwich and drank her tea slowly. She waited for Nadereh to finish hers, then asked, "What happened to make you decide to come to Canada? Did Ehsan's group arrange to send you out of the country?"

"When I was released from prison, I didn't know how to get in touch with anyone from the group, and I didn't dare ask. I didn't know anything about politics, either, but I had to get my life in order. I was in the last month of my pregnancy. I found my sister's address and stayed there until I gave birth to my baby. Then..."

She suddenly started to cry.

"I think that's enough for today," Parvaneh said.

IT IS A TEN-MINUTE WALK FROM THE BUS STOP to Parvaneh's place. The late afternoon sunshine angles through the leaves of the trees lining both sides of the street. The homes are comfortable, and the lawns are well tended. The air has a promise of colder weather to come, but for the moment the leaves on the tree in front of Parvaneh's place are still green and strong and provide cool shade for the house.

Nadereh climbs the steps to the front door. The inner door and the screen door are closed but not locked. There are no sounds inside when she enters. A painting of a woman hangs in the hallway, and a plant's tendrils climb up its frame. Leaving her shoes on feels odd—it is customary to remove them upon entering any Iranian home—but Mahan and Parvaneh are not fussy about this. She tries to ignore her discomfort as she makes her way into the living room, calling out a loud hello to announce her entry. Unexpectedly, she comes upon Mahan and Parvaneh, who spring apart, surprised at her interruption. Embarrassed, Mahan says hello and hastily retreats up the stairs.

"Sorry for disturbing you."

"No problem," Parvaneh says, fumbling to rebutton her blouse. Nadereh can see that Parvaneh's breasts are uncovered and poking through the opening in her blouse.

Parvaneh invites Nadereh to sit down, hiding her discomfort by asking, "Would you like a tea or a coffee? We have both. Or a cold drink?"

Sitting down, Nadereh says, "No thanks. I'll wait until the others arrive."

"Ferdous is the only other guest coming, right?" Parvaneh says.

"Yes, though Goodarz said he might drop by later," answers Nadereh.

Mahan returns. He has changed from shorts into jeans and a grey shirt with a white stripes. Having regained his composure, he takes a seat on the sofa.

"Sorry to have interrupted your moment of intimacy," Nadereh says. "I seem to have a flair for bursting in on people in compromising situations."

"You didn't tell me whether you wanted tea or coffee. We have beer, too," Parvaneh offers.

"I'll have a beer, if you don't mind."

"Sure, we have beer; where there is a man there's always beer."

Mahan goes to the kitchen and comes back with two bottles and a bowl of chips. He gives one of the beers to Nadereh. "What about me?" Parvaneh asks. "Did you forget about me?"

Taking a drink from the bottle, Nadereh looks over at Mahan and winks. "He could never forget you," she says.

Mahan jumps up and says, "But sweetheart, you never drink beer."

"I'm joking," Parvaneh says. "It's okay. I have to make tea, anyway."

She gets up and starts for the kitchen.

"You sit down," Mahan says. "It's my turn to serve today."

As he disappears into the kitchen, Nadereh takes another sip from her bottle, then reaches for the chips. Glancing around the room, she says, "This place looks different. It seems more spacious. Something's missing."

"I took the TV upstairs to mom's room," Parvaneh says. "She likes to watch TV in bed. Now whenever she comes to visit, we don't have to move the TV. Also, Mahasti got badly attached to the TV and spent most of her time in front of it. I did too. You can get addicted to it. And the programs—you know how they are—they're lousy! It's better this way. Now we spend more quality time together. We even speak to one another."

"What about the news?"

"We listen to the radio; it's always on. The programs are much better and the news is too."

"Good for you, living without a TV."

"Believe me, today TV is more destructive than constructive, especially for Mahasti. It's not easy to control what she absorbs."

"Have you heard anything from your mother? It's been more than a week since I've last seen her."

"She's fine. I spoke to her last night. She was asking about you."

"Is she going to be here today?"

"No, I thought it would only tire her out."

PARVANEH'S MOTHER SAT ON A STOOL in front of the washroom mirror with a cape over her shoulders. Nadereh stood behind her with a small brush in her hand. Dunking the brush into a bowl of colour, she applied it to a small section of Mother's hair. The mirror reflected Mother's tiny, fragile-looking countenance. Looking at the wrinkled face in the mirror, Nadereh saw a pensive sadness in Mother's faraway look. Parvaneh's mother made Nadereh think fondly of her own departed mother, and the chaotic life she herself had lived so far. Nadereh sometimes thought of Mother as a replacement for her own mother, even though she would never completely erase the memory of the woman who had held her lovingly in her arms as a child.

Nadereh was glad that Mother appreciated her affection. The sudden death of her own mother meant that she had never had a chance to experience this kind of relationship. As hard as she tried, she also could never remember herself or her sisters showing their mother love. As she thought about it more, she realized that the love she had for Parvaneh's mother was mixed with a kind of sympathy, which was exactly what Mother wanted.

Nadereh was looking at Mother in the mirror. "Parvaneh looks more like you than your other daughters," she said. "She has your height and eyes. Soraya and Farnaz probably resemble their father more."

Mother looked back at Nadereh in the mirror, sighed, and said, "Yes, Soraya and Farnaz take after their father's side of the family; they look like their older aunt. But Parvaneh is the same height as me. She's always been upset because she's short and slightly chubby, but her chubbiness isn't my fault. As Mahan says, she should be careful about what she eats. Well, is it my fault she's short? I got it from my parents, too."

Nadereh smiled and said, "Is it important?"

"How do I know? When you get old, and dependent to your children, you will lose your real place in the family.

But your children love you and respect you.

"Oh ... Nadereh, don't open my wounds. Are you sure they love me? When we were still in Iran and I had something of my own and I had my place in the family, yes, they loved me. I don't know if you have read *Father Goriot* or not. Your mother is lucky she's not alive to experience these times. I wouldn't want to be like *Father Goriot*."

"Who's this Father Goriot anyway?"

"*Father Goriot* is the title of a book by Balzac. I read it when I was young. My father was a man of books, and he had all of Balzac's books. Yes, Balzac was a French writer."

Applying the last drop of colour to Mother's hair, Nadereh asked, "How's the story related to your life?"

Mother looked at Nadereh in the mirror and said, "It's a story of an old man who divides his wealth among his three daughters. Before he divided his wealth, he was loved by his three daughters and each of them wanted him to live with them. But afterwards, when he had nothing left for himself and needed his daughters' care, not one of them wanted anything to do with him. Now, it's my story. I had a house in Iran and the pension of my late husband. I was financially independent from my children. Then I sold the house and gave the money to Parvaneh to immigrate with her husband. Now they have a good income, but she returns the money to her sisters and brother as their father's inheritance. If I hadn't sold the house, I would have a place to go back to. But now, here I am, unwanted, useless, and a burden. I'm not even useful to watch their children anymore; they don't need me. The three of them all have big houses, but none of them wants me around. I don't expect anything from Sohrab, with his wife, an American...."

"Wouldn't you be uncomfortable living that way? Being dependent on them? You have your own home. When you have your own home, you can do as you wish."

Mother sighed and said, "God bless the government of Canada, that gave me this small apartment with a low rent and a pension of my own. I also have some pension of my late husband in Iran, too. Thank God I don't need them financially. Yes, as you say, I'm happy with the privacy I get, but do you call a mouse hole a home? I can't invite all of them to visit me at once, now that Farnaz has a daughter-in-law and a grandchild and Soraya has a son-in-law. God save them, there is no way they could all fit in here. Neither could my friends. I've become a lonely old owl. If you didn't come to see me, no one would; I don't exist for my children and grandchildren."

Nadereh removed the cape. Mother stood up and said, "Please Nadereh, don't reopen my painful wounds. I have no choice. What can I do? Go back to Iran? I told you, I sold everything I had. I have to cope with all of this. God bless your parents; to me, you are dearer than my own children."

NADEREH FINISHES HER BEER. When Parvaneh goes upstairs, Mahan stays in the living room with Nadereh. Mahan breaks the silence; he points to the bottle in front of her and says, "How about another one?" He looks at his watch and continues, "Ms. Ferdous is late, as usual."

"You should stop her," Nadereh says. "Don't sit back and say, 'It's not my business.'"

"Is it though?" Mahan asks. "Who am I to tell her what to do?"

"Everyone says, it's not my business," Nadereh says. "I'm just a nobody, but at least I care for her."

BY THE TIME NADEREH HAD FOUND OUT about Ferdous's decision, the surgery was only a week away. Nadereh was attending a seminar at Parvaneh's workplace. After the seminar, they returned to Parvaneh's office to visit and catch up on things. When Parvaneh told Nadereh about Ferdous's decision, Nadereh said, "I can't believe it. The poor woman is finally going to stand on her own two feet."

"Not exactly. Ferdous has been depressed again. She told me her doctor has increased her medication."

"So her decision might be because of the depression?"

"I don't know, but I think she's being very unselfish and kind-hearted. You could give some thought to doing the same thing for someone."

"My situation is different from hers. As you say, she's depressed again. In my view, Ghobad and Frida are taking advantage of the poor woman." Nadereh stood up and started to pace around the room. "I don't believe that—" She stopped mid-sentence and said instead, "I'm going out for a cigarette."

Parvaneh's office was in a family resource centre located on a quiet tree-lined street. She had told Nadereh that the street brought back the memory of her father's house, which was located on a similar street, Pasteur Avenue, in Tehran. When she was growing up, she only had to cross the street to attend school. When they wanted to sell the house and immigrate, Parvaneh had told Mahan that she would miss those trees, which made a canopy of green leaves in summer, even more than her father's house, which she had so many memories of.

Nadereh sat on a bench in front of the building with her jacket on. Fall had just begun and the weather was getting cooler. Before she had smoked half of her cigarette, Parvaneh came out of the building with her coat on her shoulders. She'd sat down beside Nadereh, and said, "I thought you'd left. I don't understand why you're against Ferdous's decision. I think she's doing this just because she cares for other people. When she told me what she was going to do, I admired her for it."

Nadereh took another puff on her cigarette, and as she exhaled, she muttered under her breath, "Love for humanity!"

"You should admire her," Nadereh said sarcastically. "I'm sure anyone who hears about her decision will admire her and tell her what an unselfish person she is. But I...."

She didn't finish her sentence. She stamped out her cigarette and said goodbye to Parvaneh. Before she walked away, she added, "Parvaneh, promise me like you would to anyone you love—your flawless husband, your daughter, lovely Mahasti, or your dear mother—that you will try to talk some sense into her and to find out why she wants to do this to herself. Isn't she aware of the seriousness of the sacrifice she is making? I'll do my best, but my words don't mean anything to Ferdous. She doesn't look at me the same way she does you. Sweet, innocent Ferdous doesn't put much stock in my opinions. I'm nobody in her view, just a nothing. But you have a place in the community. You can make an impression on her."

Parvaneh placed her hand gently on Nadareh's arm and said, "I don't understand what you find problematic about her decision. She's doing a very shumane thing."

Nadereh looked directly into Parvaneh's eyes, struggling to control herself. She said angrily, "A humane thing! For someone who has control of their faculties, yes, it is a humane act, but not for Ferdous; she needs help herself. They're taking advantage of her and she doesn't know it. She believes she's doing a selfless thing, but there's no humanity in it. I spit on any humanity that Ghobad and Ibrahim represent. Doesn't Ghobad have enough money now? He could easily take Frida to another part of the world where he could buy a kidney for her. I don't understand why you're feeling sorry for Frida. They're disgusting."

"Nadereh, don't take it so badly. Frida has seen her share of misery. If you knew about her..."

"I know, I know. But has her life been any more difficult than mine has? And now, look at her, look at me. Are we in the same situation? What about poor Ferdous? Why doesn't anyone feel sorry for her? Everyone wants to use her to solve their own problems. The Iranians who are so proud of themselves, they have all forgotten about her. As Ferdous says, no one has any patience for a person with mental health issues. But it's not right to take advantage of the poor woman either."

CHAPTER 5

IN THE BACKYARD OF PARVANEH'S HOUSE, Goodarz is sitting on a bench, smoking. Parvaneh, Nadereh, and Mahan are in the kitchen. When Nadereh told Goodarz she was going to Parvaneh's house and that Ferdous was supposed to come, too, Goodarz, not one to give people unsolicited advice, asked how she planned to make Ferdous change her decision. Nadereh asked him to come with her, so he could accompany her home afterwards. She didn't want to stay overnight at Parvaneh's house and, the next morning, to have to accompany Ferdous to the hospital.

Goodarz was his parents' only child. He didn't remember too much about his father. When he was four or five, his father was sent on a work assignment to Europe—his mother hadn't known anything about it. When the group returned two weeks later, Fariborz Namdaran wasn't with them. When his mother called the company to ask about her husband, they told her Mr. Namdaran had gone on to France at the end of the job. They had also informed her that a large sum of money had been stolen from the company and that Mr. Namdaran was a suspect.

His mother, Minoo, had waited for her missing husband for years. Her father argued that she should divorce Fariborz and remarry. But she loved her husband deeply and didn't have the courage to do her father's bidding. A chartered accountant in the finance ministry, Minoo's father was able to find a job for his daughter there. He also renovated his house and installed a second-floor apartment for Minoo and her son. He loved his daughter and wanted her to be happy, but he didn't like being with Goodarz because the child reminded him of Fariborz.

Minoo waited twenty years for her husband to come back. In the meantime, Goodarz grew up and finished high school. Minoo devoted her life to him and never allowed him to lift a finger. If Minoo had not been killed in a car accident, she probably would have used all her resources to send her son to university, help him find a wife, and ensure he lived the good life.

In those years, many families tried to keep their young sons from fighting in the war with Iraq. However, Goodarz decided to go, hoping to die with honour. Being his mother's only child, and therefore exempted from military service, after she died, he was able to enlist in the army voluntarily. Although he served on the front lines, he escaped the death he wished for. When his military service ended, he still had some money left, so he was able to leave the country. He went to Turkey and applied for asylum through the United Nations. As a refugee, he travelled to Sweden, where he first overcame his drug addiction, a problem he had since he was in the army. However, he was intensely lonel, and before long he turned to drugs again. After a few months, he met Delsi, a volunteer for humanity work, and they soon married. An intelligent, lively girl, she was an experienced global traveller, the daughter of a Swedish mother and a Venezuelan father. She travelled with Goodarz to Iran where they spent a few months visiting many cities. Eventually they settled on coming to Canada.

In Canada, Delsi left Goodarz and disappeared. He divorced her while he was dating Edvina, whom he married a few months later in order to qualify for Canadian citizenship. Edvina was from Thailand and wanted a family. Together they had a daughter, but Goodarz never believed the child was his and didn't have any feelings for her. Edvina opened a fast food restaurant in downtown Toronto and wanted Goodarz to work for her full time, but his heart wasn't in it. She constantly nagged him, reminding him of his past and putting him down. Finally, he collected his meager belongings—a bag of clothing and a few books—and left. She wasted no time applying for a divorce and Goodarz obliged. He relinquished all claims, including custody and weekly visits with her daughter.

He met Nadereh on a cold and snowy winter night, when volunteers were collecting homeless people from the streets. He was taken to a shelter where Nadareh was working the night shift. They soon developed a close and deep friendship. Sometimes he imagined he was in love with her, but he warned himself to be careful—he wanted to avoid another painful relationship.

MAHAN JOINS GOODARZ AS HE IS FINISHING his cigarette. He quickly becomes absorbed by the beauty of a cardinal flitting among the branches of the cedar tree.

Standing up, Goodarz watches the bird fly away. He says, "Canada's nature amazes me."

"It amazes me, too. And I have grown to love it. I never imagined I could stay away from my country for so long. I've been here for almost a decade now."

"I don't care where I live. I don't want to be dependent on anything; it makes a slave out of me," Goodarz retorts, his voice gruff.

Mahan turns away from the tree and looks at Goodarz as he says, "All of us are slaves. Indeed, everyone is a slave to something."

Goodarz smiles, thinking to himself, *You would think like that. You're probably the slave to this house, your wife, your child, and your work.*

Nadereh opens the kitchen door and leans out into the backyard, calling, "Ferdous is here. Can you two please come in?"

Goodarz says, "You guys take care of your business, then give us a call and we'll come in."

Nadereh says, "Come in. Don't forget what I told you. Don't just sit there. We need your opinions."

Mahan jumps up and follows Goodarz into the kitchen.

Ferdous is wearing tight black pants and a striped black-and-green shirt. Her hair is light brown except for the red and gray roots. She wears dark red lipstick and light green eyeshadow, which gives her big brown eyes a sleepy appearance. The slanting rays of sunshine light up the flowerbeds—the flowers are bright red, violet, yellow, and white—and come through the kitchen window, shining on the table and the stove. Looking out, Ferdous exclaims, "What a beautiful backyard! It's really fantastic. How lovely!" She turns to Parvaneh and Mahan and says with resignation, "Life in an apartment is very boring. It's like living in a cage. Back home in Iran, my father's yard in Shemiran was like an orchard. I miss it."

Standing by the door, she turns around and says, "I prefer to sit here where it is so lively and bright. I hope you don't mind."

Nadereh speaks up. "Go ahead. Parvaneh won't charge you anything for watching her backyard." She pulls a chair close to the window and says, "Have a seat, please."

Mahan brings tea for everyone, and Parvaneh offers her visitors a tray loaded with pastries, chips, and pistachios.

Nadereh ask Ferdous, "Why are you so late? You were supposed to be here at four and it's almost five-thirty now."

Instead of answering, Ferdous gulps back the hot tea. Putting the cup in the saucer, she looks around at everyone—Nadereh and Parvaneh are all sitting on chairs, Mahan leans against the counter with a cup of tea in his hand, and Goodarz is standing by the door that leads into the backyard.

Parvaneh says, "What about you two? Don't you want to sit down? This is supposed to be an official meeting."

Mahan brings two more chairs from the dining room into the kitchen.

Nadereh declares, "Let's get down to business."

Goodarz says, "Let the poor girl relax for a minute."

Nadereh places her empty cup on the saucer and looks at Mahan, who is putting a dish of fruit on the table. She says, "You don't have to wait on us. We can serve ourselves."

Ferdous takes a big pastry, nibbles on it, and pours herself a second cup of tea. Nadereh says, "Ferdous, have you really thought about the decision you have made?"

Ferdous's hand stops on its way to her mouth. "What do you mean?"

Parvaneh says, "She means about donating your kidney."

Ferdous ignores Parvaneh's question and instead says, "I'm going to tell you something funny. When I was getting dressed to come here, Ladan called me. Guess what she wanted?"

Nobody says anything. Ferdous continues, "I'm sure none of you can guess."

Nadereh declares, "Well, tell us. But remember, we are here for a reason, not just for you to tell us riddles."

"Wait a minute, my dear. You're really impatient."

"You didn't answer me," Nadereh says seriously. "Tell us truthfully, did Ghobad force you to make this decision about your kidney?"

Ferdous pushes away the dish of half-eaten pastry. She stares at Nadereh as though she doesn't understand what she's saying, and asks, "Can I go to the washroom?"

Parvaneh answers, "Sure. You know where they are: one upstairs and one in the basement."

Ferdous slowly walks out of the kitchen.

Parvaneh glances up at the clock and says, "I'd better get us something else to eat. It's getting dark." She sets the table and then starts to prepare a light dinner.

During dinner, no one speaks. It is silent around the table except for the sound of people eating or pouring drinks, and the noise of forks and knives hitting the plates. Ferdous is quiet, playing with the potato salad on her plate and not really eating. She toys with her bread and then the small scoop of pasta that Parvaneh has just added to her plate.

"Why don't you eat?" Parvaneh asks. "Don't you like it? Or have you already eaten?"

Ferdous nibbles at her food like a child obeying her mother's command. She says, "See, I'm eating. You made too much and there is so much to choose from...."

They eat silently for a few minutes, but then Ferdous says, "When I went to the washroom in the basement, I looked around down there. It's nice and bright, and you've finished it very nicely. There is a bath, bedroom, and a living room with a small kitchen...."

She stops talking and looks around. Nobody says anything. They look down at their plates to avoid looking at each other. Ferdous continues, hesitantly. "I was wondering if I could rent your basement. I really like your house. It's even better than Ghobad and Frida's. And their house has ten or twenty rooms. You can get lost in it. They have a room in the basement for their guests, and I stayed there overnight once. But their basement is dark like a grave. They said it was quieter down there, but I could hear their footsteps above me. Their swimming pool was beside the room I slept in, and I kept hearing odd noises coming from there. It was as if ghosts were swimming in the pool. To tell you the truth, I was scared to death and I woke up several times in the middle of the night. The next time they asked me to stay, I refused. I was afraid they would send me to the basement again."

Nadereh says, "Why didn't you tell them that you were afraid?"

Ferdous ignores Nadereh. Staring into space, she says, "I was asking whether Parvaneh and Mahan would rent me their basement. I'm really sick and tired of living in an apartment. My depression is mostly because I live in that filthy apartment. My doctor said that if I change my living conditions, I'll feel better. You don't know what a disgusting place it is. You can't imagine what kind of tenants live there. They don't care about other people, or about keeping the place clean. There's always a bad smell in the hallway. Tonight, it occurred to me—would it be possible to move into your place?"

Her words are imploring. She looks from Parvaneh to Mahan, waiting for an answer, but they give her a puzzled look and say nothing. She looks at Nadereh and then Goodarz and asks, "What do you think? Isn't it a good idea?"

Nadereh has finished eating. She gets up, puts her plate in the sink, and says, "I'm going out for a cigarette." She looks at Goodarz and asks, "What about you? Do you want to smoke?" He looks like someone who has just been awakened from a deep sleep. He shakes himself and stands up. Nadereh turns to Mahan and declares, "Don't touch the dishes. I've promised to wash them."

Offended, Parvaneh chides Nadereh. "Go and have your cigarette. Don't worry about the dishes."

Ferdous is still sitting with her head down, playing with a piece of bread in her hand when Nadereh and Goodarz return to the kitchen. She finally raises her head, and looks at Nadereh for a long time, then at Goodarz. She seems lost in thought. Nadereh is sure Parvaneh's answer has been negative and that Ferdous is upset.

Parvaneh is spooning leftover food in containers and putting them into the fridge, muttering under her breath, "Most of the food was untouched. No one ate anything."

Nobody says anything. A painful silence settles over the group.

"It's time for some tea and cake," Parvaneh declares.

Nadereh says, "Do you want to make us burst? Ever since we've arrived, all we've done is eat. We were supposed to talk about a very important issue—an issue of life and death. It seems that you don't even want to start."

"It's not me that has something to say," Parvaneh answers. "Ferdous doesn't seem to want to talk about it. She's already made her decision. She isn't a child. If there is something she wants to discuss, she should say so."

Nadereh starts to say, "She's not a child, but she's stup..."

then stops halfway through the word she is about to utter. She looks at Ferdous, who is chewing her nails.

Ferdous says, "I'm sick and tired of my life."

Her eyes are fixed on Nadereh. She puts her arms on the table, lowers her head onto her arms and sobs. The sound of the telephone drowns out Ferdous's sobs.

Parvaneh hurries to the telephone and mumbles, "That must be Mahasti, my poor baby. She wants to come back home." She lifts the receiver. The look on her face changes into a smile. After a few words, she says goodbye and puts the phone down. Turning around, she smiles brightly and says, "It was Ghobad. He told me that Frida is running a fever and she can't have the operation until her fever goes away. It won't be necessary for Ferdous to go to the hospital right away."

CHAPTER 6

PARVANEH AWAKENS TO THE SOUND of the telephone. Mahan isn't in bed, and she thinks he might have gone to answer the phone. The ringing is incessant and disturbs the womblike coziness of the bedroom. Parvaneh's thoughts turn to Mahasti as she fumbles for the receiver. She is relieved to hear Ghobad's voice and asks quickly, "How's Frida?" Ghobad's reply is laboured, and she can tell he is straining to control his emotions. He says in a trembling voice, "Frida's gone." At first Parvaneh misinterprets Ghobad's words. She is about to ask, "Where?" when she hears him sobbing on the other end of the line and realizes what he means. She recalls his call from the previous night, saying that Frida was running a fever. Parvaneh's confusion is quickly dissipating as she returns to full wakefulness. Ghobad sobs as she asks, "What happened?"

"Frida's gone. She's gone forever," Ghobad mumbles, and he cries bitterly.

Parvaneh says, "I don't understand. How could it have happened so fast?"

Ghobad seems not to have heard the question. He chokes back his tears and says, "Excuse me for waking you so early in the morning. I wanted to talk to Mahan. If...."

Parvaneh calls for her husband, panic in her voice. She remembers they argued last night after Nadereh and Goodarz had left. This time she calls louder: "Mahan!"

She hears her voice echoing in the stairwell. Still, there is no answer. She tells Ghobad, "Hold the line please, I'll call him. He's not in the bedroom, and I don't know where he is. Perhaps...." She climbs out of the bed, and tucking the phone between her ear and shoulder, she opens the door to the bathroom and peers inside. Mahan isn't there. She calls him again, and, talking to herself, wonders where he is. To Ghobad she says, "I don't understand. What's happened to Frida?"

"She passed away an hour ago," he replies. "The doctor says it was a stroke."

Parvaneh is stunned. "No, that's not possible." Still in disbelief, she says, "This can't have happened."

"Sorry, sorry," Ghobad mumbles. "I have to go. If Mahan..." There is further mumbling, then Ghobad whispers, "Sorry, I have to go," and cuts the connection.

Parvaneh stares at the phone in her hand. She can't believe what she's just heard. She wants to call the hospital, but she can't remember the number. Slowly she goes down the stairs, the phone still in her hand. In the living room, Ferdous is sleeping on the sofa.

Last night, Parvaneh tried to wake her up and send her to the guest room, but she refused to go. She has the blanket draped over her, but half of the blanket has almost completely slid to the floor, and Ferdous's head is bent at an impossible angle. Traces of the lipstick she had smeared over her mouth remain. Her breathing is laboured, like she is stuffed up from a cold. Mahan is still nowhere to be found. The humming of the fridge is the only sound to disturb the early morning silence. Glancing at the clock on the stove, she sees it is six-fifteen. She opens the door to the backyard. The weather is damp and cool, and the sky is grey. Mahan isn't out there either. Her anger at him starts to return. She still has the cordless phone with her. She dials Nadereh's number. After a few rings, it goes to her voicemail. Nadereh's greeting is short, like the sentences she sometimes doesn't finish. Parvaneh mumbles, "Damn!" Surprised at her vehemence toward the recording and her growing anger toward Nadereh, she waits for the voicemail message to finish. Coldly, she states, "Frida passed away. And...." She doesn't know what else to say. She is halfway down the basement stairs when she asks herself, "Why am I going down here?" But she continues to descend. The basement is dark and gloomy, but Parvaneh can see Mahan asleep under the basement window, on the leather sofa they picked up at a garage sale.

Quietly, Parvaneh approaches him and puts her hand on his head. When Mahan opens his eyes, Parvaneh asks, "Have you been sleeping here all night? Didn't you hear the telephone?"

He doesn't respond.

"Ghobad just called," Parvaneh says. "He said that Frida's gone. I didn't believe him. I was half asleep. It's true, though. He wanted to speak to you. What are you doing down here?"

Mahan stands up. He glances out the window and says, "It's already morning."

Parvaneh still has the telephone in her hand. She says, "We have to go to the hospital."

Ignoring Parvaneh, Mahan starts up the stairs, and she follows him. Mahan slips into the washroom and closes the door firmly behind him. Parvaneh tries the handle of the door; it is locked. Inside there is the noise of running water. She returns to the bedroom and sits on the edge of the bed. She replays last night's argument in her mind. She remembers the looks Mahan had exchanged with Nadereh, and she feels a twinge of jealousy. She tries not to allow her mind to wander along those lines.

Back in the bedroom, Mahan continues to ignore Parvaneh and goes toward the closet. Parvaneh is sitting on the edge of the bed; she's hurt by his behaviour and she doesn't want to accept that he is still annoyed with her. In earlier days, it was always Mahan who made the first overtures after a conflict; he would always say that when two people can talk and understand each other, there was no reason to argue or fight. *Our annoyance with each other has never lasted more than a few hours, so why can't he step forward and break the ice this time?*

Last night's argument comes to her mind again. Why didn't she stay in the kitchen to talk to Mahan? Why, instead of confronting him, did she act like a spoiled child, and run off to bed and pretend to fall asleep? Why does he blame her? Is it her fault that she wants to help people? She wants to help Ferdous but she cannot allow her to live in their basement apartment. Ferdous gives her enough trouble, and if she comes to live with them under the same roof, she fears that Ferdous would become a real burden. Mahan should have understood her feelings, but instead he said she wasn't genuine about helping people. He accused her of living a lie. He called her a hypocrite, and said he admired Nadereh and Goodarz, who were honest and generous to people and to themselves as well.

Thinking about last night makes her feel angry and ashamed of herself. However, she eases her own guilty feelings by reminding herself that whenever Mahan is angry or upset with he, he always sulks for a while, and it isn't uncommon for him to not sleep in the same bed with her. As Mahan is leaving the bedroom, she says, "Wait. I want to come with you."

Without looking at her, he states, "You and Ferdous can come later. I have to go and see what Ghobad needs. He might...." He leaves without finishing his sentence.

When Mahan closes the front door behind him, Parvaneh bursts into tears. She can't figure out whether she is crying for herself or for Frida. But her thoughts are mostly occupied by Mahan and Nadereh. She has a feeling that Mahan is leaving and not coming back. Angrily she says aloud, "That bitch! I'm not going to give her the satisfaction of...."

She is once again surprised at her vehemence. She mumbles to herself, "Nothing happened. Why am I mad at Nadereh? It should be Ferdous I'm mad at." She hurries down the stairs. Ferdous is still asleep on the sofa. She sleeps with her head resting on her arm, her hair draped across the side of her face. Her mouth is half open, and she snores lightly. For a moment, Parvaneh looks at Ferdous, not knowing whether to wake her and thinking to herself, "*What's she still doing here? Should I get rid of her? If Ferdous hadn't been here, I could have gone with Mahan.*" It crosses her mind to leave Ferdous on the couch and just get in the car to follow Mahan. But she doesn't really want to go to the hospital; she just wants to talk to him. She still can't believe that Frida is dead. It is as if she is dreaming. She imagines when Mahan returns he will saying something like, "Ghobad likes to make mountains out of molehills." Then she remembers Ghobad sobbing on the phone.

She goes to the living room and walks toward the sofa where Ferdous is sleeping. A quiet moan escapes from Ferdous's lips. Parvaneh sits on the edge of the sofa, reaches out, and gently shakes Ferdous's shoulder, saying, "Ferdous, honey, wake up, we have to go."

Ferdous doesn't move. Her moaning turns back into snoring. Parvaneh shakes her and tries again, a little louder this time. "Ferdous!" Ferdous wakes up and looks at Parvaneh through sleepy eyes. She says nothing; she is confused and disoriented. Parvaneh says, "Sorry to disturb you, but…"

Parvaneh is not sure whether Ferdous is fully awake. Parvaneh stares at her closely and wonders if she should tell her about Frida's death. *Frida's death?*

Parvaneh abruptly gets up and goes into the kitchen, tears coursing down her face. She remembers Frida and her magical dancing feet—how she could thrill everyone! She climbs back upstairs to get dressed. She thinks of leaving Ferdous at home. She has to accept the fact that Frida is gone.

Back in the living room, Ferdous is sitting up and staring into space. When Parvaneh comes downstairs again, she says, "I had a dream that there was a fire in your house. Mahan and Mahasti died in the fire, but you were screaming and crying when they rescued you. The sound of the fire truck woke me up. Did you hear anything?"

Parvaneh sits beside Ferdous and prepares to break the news to her.

Ferdous looks at Parvaneh and asks, "Do you think that Nadereh is right? Am I making a mistake? Last night I dreamed they took both my kidneys and I was going to die. Do you think...?"

Parvaneh puts her hand on Ferdous's shoulder and says, "My dear..."

"Is something wrong?"

"We have to go to the hospital. I'm not sure yet. I don't know anything. We just have to go to the hospital. Mahan's already gone and we have to go too."

"If nothing's wrong, why are you dressed all in black?" Ferdous asks.

She breaks down, suddenly dropping her head onto the pillow. Sobbing loudly, she cries, "I don't want to give my kidney to Frida. Nadereh is right. They don't care about me, they only want my kidney."

Angrily, Parvaneh says, "Sweetheart, you don't have to."

Ferdous sits up straight and says, "What's wrong with you? You call me sweetheart all the time. I hate you, I hate all of you. Nadereh is my only true friend. All of you want to use me."

Parvaneh stands up and says, "Are you coming with me or not? Hurry up. It's already too late."

Ferdous calms down and wipes the tears from her eyes. She gets up and goes to the washroom. A few minutes later she returns, her hair still messy and the smear of lipstick still on her lips; she looks even more pitiful than usual.

Parvaneh says, "Couldn't you even comb your hair and wash your face? We're supposed to..." She doesn't continue. She's wondering how to get rid of Ferdous. Frida's death overshadows her thoughts. Parvaneh feels even angrier than she did last night after the argument with Mahan. She isn't sure if it's because Mahan slept in the basement, or because Ferdous is still in her house, or whether Frida's sudden death is causing her to lose control. It is as if a voice inside her is warning her that with Frida's death, the sanctuary that is her home is threatened, too.

Absentmindedly, she leaves the house and climbs into her car, then leans her head back and closes her eyes for a while, wondering what she will do with Ferdous when she reaches the hospital. *I'll leave her with Nadereh,* she thinks, then mumbles out loud, "I have to go to Farnaz's place and get Mahasti, too." The thought of Mahasti brings a smile to her face. *My poor baby, I was too busy to get her last night. Tonight I'll make it up to her. We'll all be together again, Mahan, Mahasti, and me. He is right. I shouldn't concern myself with other people's affairs. I can't do anything for them anyway; I just cause more trouble for myself.*

She parks the car close to the hospital. Ferdous has fallen asleep again in the back seat. Parvaneh jerks open the car door to wake her up. Ferdous opens her eyes and looks at Parvaneh, puzzled, as if she doesn't know where she is, then slowly gets out of the car. Parvaneh takes her arm and leads her into the hospital. Ferdous asks, "Where are you taking me? I don't want to donate my kidney to Frida. I wish she was dead."

Parvaneh drags her along and says, "You don't have to donate your kidney. Don't you remember last night when Ghobad called and said that she wasn't going to have surgery today?"

When they reach the hospital entrance, Ferdous suddenly stops and says, "I'll wait here until you have a visit with Frida and come back down. Tell her I have a cold and I don't want to give it to her." She turns and walks toward the coffee shop.

Waiting for the elevator, Parvaneh suddenly remembers she doesn't even know which floor Frida is on. She worries that if she goes back to the reception area to find out, Ferdous might see her and change her mind about coming with her. Instead, she shrugs her shoulders and steps into the elevator, gets out at the first stop and makes her way to the nursing station. The young woman behind the desk sends her to another ward. At the end of the hallway, Parvaneh sees a crowd standing around a door. As she strolls toward the group, she recognizes Ibrahim and Sussan among them. She can't see whether Mahan is in the crowd. As she is searching for him, Ghobad comes out of the room. His son and daughter are hanging onto him on both sides as if they are afraid to let him go. Parvaneh hugs the three of them and sniffles. Not allowing herself to cry, she wipes the tears from her eyes and asks Ibrahim about Mahan. Nadereh isn't there either. She fights back the thoughts that are taking shape in her mind. When the crowd leaves and Ghobad and the children are alone, Parvaneh steps close to him and whispers, "Mahan came to the hospital early this morning. Have you seen him yet?"

Ghobad says, "He was here. But he didn't stay long. He didn't say whether he'd be back or not."

The idea that he may have gone to Nadereh's is eating away at her. Ghobad asks, "Have you heard from Ferdous? She told me that she was going to spend the night with you before the surgery."

"Yes, she stayed with us. I brought her to the hospital with me. She went to the coffee shop and I hurried on up."

Another group arrives, and Ghobad greets them sadly, accepting their condolences. Back in the lobby, Parvaneh doesn't see Ferdous anywhere. Glad to be rid of her, she goes to her car and calls home on her cellphone. The call goes to voicemail. Then she dials Nadereh's number and gets her answering message. She gets into the car and drives directly to Richmond Hill.

Hassan invites her in and follows her into the kitchen. It is nine in the morning, but no one is there.

"Isn't anyone up yet?" she asks.

Farnaz comes into the kitchen, wearing a colourful robe with big red, yellow, and orange flowers over her nightgown. Her hair is pulled back and tied at the back of her head. When Parvaneh sees Farnaz, she covers her face with both her hands and starts to sob. Farnaz rushes to her and hugs her close, asking, "What's wrong, honey? Where's Mahan?"

Parvaneh wipes the tears from her eyes and answers, "It's all my fault. Mahan disappeared early this morning. I'm not sure if he went with that girl...."

Then she notices her mother has come into the kitchen and is staring at her questioningly. "What's wrong?" she asks. "Why are you crying?"

Parvaneh looks at her mother and says, "This morning, Ghobad called and said Frida passed away."

Mother gives her a shocked look and says, "Passed away? No! When? The poor woman!"

Farnaz says, "Wasn't she supposed to have surgery today? Wasn't Ferdous donating her kidney?"

"She never got a chance to have the surgery," Parvaneh says. "Last night Nadereh *khanum* tried to convince Ferdous not to donate her kidney, but in the end the poor woman didn't even last till this morning."

"You shouldn't condemn Nadereh just because Frida died," Mother objects.

Parvaneh, ignoring Mother, says, "I'd told Ferdous to come to my place and spend the night before the surgery. I asked Nadereh to accompany Ferdous to the hospital, too, just so she wouldn't be by herself."

Farnaz says, "This is your own fault. How many times have Mother and I told you not to get mixed up in other people's business? You didn't listen to us."

Parvaneh interrupts her angrily. "Do you think I like it? It's my job."

Hassan, who has been standing back, not saying a word, speaks up. "At least you shouldn't bring your job home with you. I have to tolerate my wife's job at home and put up with her customers, but you don't have to."

Farnaz turns and looks at Hassan, who still has his coffee in his hand and is leaning on the counter. His hair is dishevelled and his striped white shirt is stretched over his belly. She says, "I have to work from home. If you earned more money, I wouldn't have to work so hard to cater to people's high expectations."

Mother asks Parvaneh, "So what caused Nadereh and Mahan to become Layli and Majnoon overnight and run away?"

Parvaneh sips her tea and says, "Suddenly, Mahan seems to have changed. Last night he slept in the basement."

Mother says, "That's it? The way you were crying, I thought that Mahan had divorced you and run away with Nadereh to the other side of the planet. My sweet daughter, don't imagine such bad things. That girl is capable of anything, except stealing your husband. What's so bad about her? So, she is pretty. She is young. And she is lovely. I am a woman and even I can see how beautiful and lovely she is. But I'm old enough to know people, and to see through them. She's an honest girl and I am certain that she would never even think about stealing a friend's husband."

Hassan laughs loudly and says, "Good for you, Grandma. You too!"

Just then, Mahasti appears in the kitchen door. Parvaneh opens her arms and her daughter throws herself into them.

CHAPTER 7

IT'S ALMOST ONE IN THE MORNING when Nadereh and Goodarz leave Parvaneh's house. A cool breeze is blowing, and it feels refreshing after the stuffy house. A few stars sparkle through the light cloud cover. A cloud blots out the pale moonlight, lending a slight gloominess to the night sky, which reflects the light from the sleeping city. They walk without saying a word, both of them lost in the privacy of their thoughts. They wait at the bus stop in silence, but after fifteen minutes, they give up and start to walk. Finding the subway shut down for the night, they continue east along Bloor Street.

Their shared silence hints at the anger they are both keeping locked inside themselves. Of the two, Nadereh appears to be the angrier, while Goodarz feels mostly ashamed of himself. He keeps thinking, "*Why should I get involved? I'm not even a friend. Why should I waste my time listening to their problems?*" He is angry at himself for coming, but he's also mad at Nadereh for suggesting that he accompany her this evening. He has only met Ferdous a few times, and he doesn't exactly know her. To him she always seemed to be a pitiful person, always looking for sympathy from others. When Parvaneh and Mahan turned down her request, her reaction only increased the pity and disgust he felt for her. He regrets allowing himself to become involved in the whole business. Nadereh is a loser too, he thinks. *Why does she get involved in other people's problems?* He suspects that she's only looking to gain something for herself from meddling in other people's affairs. He also noticed that Nadereh seemed to be trying to attract Mahan's attention, and he wonders if this is why she can't leave them all well enough alone. But he isn't entirely sure that this is true. Maybe he only imagined it.

They walk side by side past the dimly lit shops. Goodarz says, "I think we're getting close to High Park."

Nadereh is starting to come around. "Why don't we go to High Park and watch the sunrise?" she suggests.

Goodarz smiles and answers, "You don't seem to take anything seriously."

Indifferently, Nadereh says, "Maybe I'm ignorant. When you have been slapped around your entire life, nothing seems important or serious to you anymore. After a while being slapped just becomes part of your life."

Goodarz stares at her for a moment and says, "Nadereh, just accept that no one wants to listen to you. Ferdous knows what she's doing. Her outlook is more mature than yours is. Believe me, this is all a game and she doesn't need your advice. You're just wasting your time."

Nadereh stops walking. She puts her hand on Goodarz's arm and says, "You don't know Ferdous, do you?"

It is a rhetorical question, as if she is telling Goodarz, *"Don't go there.... I feel sorry enough for myself right now without you adding your two cents."*

They reach the entrance to High Park. A little further on, there is a bench under a street lamp. Nadereh sits down. "Ahhh, this is good." She lays her head against the back of the bench, sighs deeply, and says, "My head is pounding."

Goodarz stands beside her. "Nadereh, let me give you my last bit of advice."

She lifts her head up, opens her eyes, and asks, "Well?"

He wants to talk about something that has been bothering him for a few months now, but he's worried that bringing it up would invade Nadereh's privacy. He hesitates for few moments and then says, "Let's leave this city. You and me and these people..."

Nadereh sits up. "What do you mean by 'these people'?"

Goodarz turns away and stares off into the darkness before answering. "I could never be comfortable with these people. They're drowning in their sorrows, trapped like insects in a spider's web. Get away from Ferdous; leave her alone. Think about yourself. How much more do you think you can put up with?"

"I don't need your advice!" Nadereh snaps. "Stop it now. I've had enough of this conversation."

"Remember what I'm telling you now. Your advice won't do anyone any good. You'll be the only one who loses."

"When have I ever said that I've got the answers to other people's problems? If I had all the answers, I would have been able to help you."

"I don't need anyone's help," Goodarz says heatedly. "I've never asked for anything. All that free advice is rubbish. I don't give a damn for people like Parvaneh, Mahan, and Ferdous. I feel ashamed sitting at the same table with them."

Nadereh's eyes flash as she tries to control herself. "Well," she says calmly, "Mister high and mighty, what happened that made you stoop so low as to associate with us?"

Without thinking, Goodarz says, "I wanted to be sure of something and now I am."

"What?"

"Forget it; it's nothing. As I said before, I wanted to find out if you could change Ferdous's mind and get her back on her feet." He pauses, then recites a poem that has just come to his mind.

"Ah...
I would have been happier
To be born an insect,
Or maybe a leaf,
Or maybe ... nothing!"

"Spare me," Nadereh pleads. "I don't have the patience to put up with your blathering."

"Then let me cheer you up with a story."

Nadereh sits there silently.

Goodarz continues. "It's a story that might make you feel better and forget about everything."

"Go ahead and tell me your story. If it's boring, I'll ignore you and lie down on this bench to sleep."

Impatiently, he asks, "Are you going to listen or not?"

She looks at him, curious now. "Well, what are you waiting for?"

He says, "I..."

He stops for a moment. The noise of a train in the distance breaks the silence of the night. Nadereh says, "Well, what happened to your story?"

"I killed my mother," Goodarz says. Then he stops.

He doesn't really know why he wants to talk about his mother's death, but something compels him to do so. He hasn't thought about it for a long time, but all of a sudden the horror of the accident comes back to him. It seems like it happened just a few days ago, and he desperately needs to talk about it with Nadereh. He wonders why he didn't mention it before. He'd already told her that his mother died in an accident, but he never mentioned that he was driving the car. Now he is determined to tell her the whole story.

Nadereh sits expectantly, waiting for Goodarz to continue. The whispering breeze is the only sound. He clears his throat and asks, "Did you hear me? I killed my mother."

Collecting herself, Nadereh looks at Goodarz. He is standing in front of her, waiting for her to say something, and her big eyes fill with fear. She quickly shakes off her apprehension, laughs loudly, and says, "Are you serious? Do you think I'm such a child that you can tell me a story and I'll forget about what happened tonight?"

Goodarz repeats, "I killed my mother. Believe me."

"I can't believe you. Don't make a fool of me or yourself."

Goodarz turns away from her and says in a louder voice, "I killed my mother. Why don't you want to believe me?"

This time Nadereh laughs mirthlessly and says, "Are you trying to amuse me? You don't have a funny story, so now you're making up something about your poor mother."

Goodarz shouts, "Nadereh, do you want to listen to me or not?"

Still furious, Nadereh answers, "Well, if it is true, then why are you telling me? If you really killed your mother, what are you doing here? Didn't you break the law?"

Goodarz laughs loudly. "Law? The law is bullshit! Besides, the law had nothing to do with it. I..."

Wearily, Naderh says. "You're just exaggerating!" And after a while she says, "You told me before that it was an accident. Go on, but keep it short."

Goodarz says, "Yes, it was an accident, but..."

"There is no way an accident would be considered a deliberate murder even if you were found guilty."

"So, you don't want to listen."

"Not if it was an accident. I'm not in the mood to hear your story. Instead, tell me why everything looks so bleak. Why can't I feel happy? How come I feel like I want to die?"

Goodarz sits beside her and looks into her face. Raising his voice, he says, "Listen to me. I thought I could tell you about my pain, a burden that I carry with me every day of my life. My mother is with me day and night. I see her everywhere. She's in the car mirror, looking back at me. Grandfather is sitting beside me in the passenger seat, giving me orders: 'Don't drive too fast, don't pass that car, turn left, turn right, look to your right, look to your left, do this, do that. Look for a job, or continue your education. Take care of your mother, take her to a movie, tell her to marry again. Tell her she is wasting her life. Tell her your bastard father, who disappeared and never gave a damn about his wife and son, isn't worth a dime. You should be careful, too, or else you might turn out just like him.'

"He talked and talked and talked. I don't know what happened to him that day. It might be because we were coming back from visiting his younger daughter—I mean my aunt—who was living a comfortable life in a big house in Rasht. She had a wealthy husband who cared about his wife and his children. Grandfather always drove me crazy with his nagging. Grandmother told him several times to stop, but Mom didn't say anything. Looking in her eyes in the mirror, I could tell that she was pleading with me not to say anything, to be patient, to put up with it. I could see in her eyes that she hated him talking to me this way; it made her miserable. And me, I was eaten up with anger and desperation. I felt like I wanted a car to hit me and kill me. I was so absorbed by my anger that I didn't see the big truck passing a car on the opposite side of the road. When I realized what was happening, it was too late for us to pass the truck or to slow down and let it pass. Our car was thrown right into the ditch.

"Grandfather died instantly. Grandmother suffered many fractures, and my left arm was broken. But at first it seemed like nothing had happened to my mother. She was thrown out of the car. I struggled out and found her in the ditch. When she saw me, she sat down and said, 'My sweetheart, my poor baby, what happened?' I was dizzy, and the pain in my arm was excruciating. Then I saw my mother lie down, as though she needed a rest. I called out to her, but she didn't answer me. I called again, louder this time. Someone stopped to help. First, he shook my mother and said, 'Lady!' There was no answer. I don't know what happened next. I screamed and cried for my mother. An ambulance came and took all of us to the hospital. I heard them saying that my mother and grandfather were dead but that my grandmother was still alive. Grandmother was in the hospital for a few months, and then she died too."

The leaves on the trees stir in the early morning breeze as if they are agitated by Goodarz's story. Suddenly there is a commotion of chirping birds. Nadereh stands up. The first rays of sunlight brighten the eastern sky, while the few stars still visible flicker in the west. Nadereh looks at Goodarz and says sadly, "We have been sitting here for a long time. I'm tired, now. Let's go home and get some rest." She walks languidly toward the park entrance.

Goodarz walks beside her. "So, don't you have anything else to say?" he asks.

"What can I say?"

They reach Bloor Street. The traffic in the street is starting to increase. A truck growls by them as they walk eastward. Nadereh stops suddenly. "I can't walk any longer," she says. She looks back to see a taxi approaching, and asks, "Do you have any money? I want to take a taxi."

Without waiting for him to answer, she lifts her arm and the cab brakes beside them. When they get home, Nadereh throws herself on the sofa in the living room that serves as Goodarz's bed. Goodarz goes to washroom to wash his face and brush his teeth. By the time he comes out, Nadereh has gone to her bedroom and closed the door.

He was hoping that she might fall in love with him, but he realizes now that it is time for him to move on. He takes his meager belongings and leaves the apartment quietly. At the door, he remembers he should write a note. He leaves it on the table and walks out, closing the door quietly. He slides the key under the door, removing any temptation to return. At a coffee shop, he buys coffee and a muffin, but neither has any taste.

When he reaches the bus terminal, he remembers that he doesn't have enough money. He opens his wallet and finds the credit card that Nadereh gave him. *I'll deposit the money in her account when I get to Vancouver,* he tells himself. The bus is almost ready to leave. He climbs on the bus and goes straight to the back, taking a seat in the last row. When the bus reaches the highway, he leans his head against the back of the seat and closes his eyes. Silently, he recites a poem:

It is always the same,
The unknown road ahead,
And unwanted love behind,
Left beside a forgotten trail!

HE HAD MET NADEREH IN A SHELTER for the homeless. It was a bitter winter night, and when he entered, he was covered with snow from head to toe. Nadereh was sitting at the reception desk. As she lifted her head and saw him, she smiled a welcome and cheerfully asked, "Hi, can I help you?"

Recognizing her accent, Goodarz asked quietly, "Are you Iranian?"

Nadereh's eyes, shining in her face like two black rubies, became even bigger in surprise, and she asked, "Well, yes, but how can I help you?"

Her two big eyes in her round, charming face were staring back at Goodarz. He stood mesmerized under their spell for a moment. The fact that she was Iranian somehow made him even more tongue-tied.

Nadereh smiled. "No place to go?"

Goodarz was still staring at her. "Not exactly. But..."

"Tell you the truth, we're full here tonight, but if you need a place to sleep"—she continued without waiting for him to speak—"I might be able to find you a place in another shelter." But there was no space available anywhere, so Goodarz wound up spending the whole night sitting on a wooden bench in the hallway, talking to Nadereh.

Giving him a mug of tea, she asked, "You told me you aren't homeless, so why did you come to a shelter?"

Goodarz hesitated before saying, "My roommate disappeared today, and he took the keys with him." He sipped his tea, then put the mug on the bench.

"Haven't you got your own key?" she asked, then changed the subject. "How about dinner? If you haven't eaten, there might be some—"

"I had dinner. I had the key, too, but I left it in my room."

"What about a job? Are you working or..."

Goodarz managed to hide his discomfort. He answered, "I have a job."

Nadereh's expression seemed to say *I wasn't born yesterday* but instead she asked, "What do you do?"

"I write poetry." He was surprised that the answer had just slipped out. He hadn't intended to say this, but Nadereh's eyes seemed to inspire his poetic nature.

She burst out laughing, just as Salima, her co-worker, leaned in. She had intended to tell Nadereh that she was leaving, since it was the end of her shift, but instead she muttered something to herself in English and left abruptly. Nadareh ignored her. Turning to Goodarz, she quipped, "You're kidding, right?"

"Yes, I was just putting you on. Really, I work temporary jobs."

Nadereh didn't ask anything else.

For three consecutive nights, it was the same, and every morning, he walked Nadereh home. They were so busy talking, they didn't seem to feel the bitter cold nor realize how far they were walking.

"What are you going to do when you get home?"

"What am I going to do? I am going to brush my teeth and then go to bed. Haven't you noticed I was awake all night long? How about you? You don't have anywhere to go. What are you going to do?"

"Me? It depends. If I can't find any work, I'll go to the library or maybe to a movie...."

"So when do you sleep? And where do you sleep? I haven't seen you sleep at all these past three nights."

"I can find some places, maybe in the theatre or at a mall or in the library. There's always a cozy place somewhere."

"What about your friend? Is he gone forever?"

"Gone forever."

"I never really found out what you do."

"I work for a company."

"What do you do for them? Are you a manager?"

"Do you think I'm cut out to be a manager? I'm good at distributing flyers—I'm an expert in that field. I work two or three days a week, and sometimes I make deliveries as a courier; I can get by on that."

"Why don't you rent a room for yourself?"

"I should do it, but the last three nights with you—"

She interrupted him. "These last three nights were exceptions. Because the weather was so cold, my supervisor didn't object to you staying in the reception area. Last night he said that we can't go over the shelter's legal capacity. Also, you are Iranian and you talk to me in Farsi, so he thinks you're my friend. Now that the weather is getting warmer and the snow is starting to melt, you need to find a place for yourself."

"You mean I can't enjoy your company tonight?"

"Sure, why not? But not in the shelter."

"Where then?"

"Somewhere else, maybe a coffee shop." They had reached Nadereh's place.

"Won't you invite me in?"

"Not now. I'm very sleepy."

"Where can I see you later?"

Nadereh waited for a moment. She stamped her feet on the ground to clean the snow from her boots and said, "Tonight my shift starts at eleven. We can see each other in the evening."

"Where?"

"In the coffee shop at Yonge and Queen."

WHEN NADEREH HAD ARRIVED, Goodarz was sitting at a table with a cup of coffee; he had a book of poetry by Baudelaire on the table. She went straight over to him and asked, "Do you want to have something to eat?"

"No, thank you."

"Don't be bashful. Have you eaten anything today?"

"I had a coffee. That's enough for me. Thanks anyway."

Nadereh went to the counter and came back with another coffee and two muffins. Without removing her coat, she sat down and picked up Goodarz's book. "Poetry! In English! Your English must be excellent."

"If I understood every other line of it, I'd be happy."

He took the book from Nadereh and read a poem entitled "Benediction."

She listened in silence. When he was finished, Nadereh said, "Now, translate it for me. I didn't get a word."

Goodarz translated the poem in a few sentences, then laughed.

"What's so funny? Are you laughing at my stupidity?"

Goodarz wanted to say that the poem mirrored his life story, but he didn't. Instead he stared into Nadereh's big, black eyes and said, "Do you know that you have the most beautiful eyes? I have been to many places and seen many beautiful women, but—"

"I really must tell you I don't like this kind of cheap compliment."

Closing the book, Goodarz tried to hide his awkwardness. "Do you call a simple fact a 'cheap compliment'?"

Nadereh said seriously, "Get those thoughts out of your mind. Do you think that your cheap compliments will get you any closer to jumping into bed with me?"

"What makes you imagine that I want to sleep with you?"

"Do you think I am some silly thirteen- or fourteen-year-old kid, Mr. Poet? I want you to think of me as a wise and worldly woman. Do not insult my intelligence. Otherwise you might as well be on your way."

Goodarz had an apologetic smile on his face. The thought that Nadereh might get up and leave scared him. "Why are you angry with me?" he implored. "We're two grown adults, having a mature discussion. It isn't something to be ashamed of."

"I know. But you should be careful"—The words came out without her thinking—"You might be carrying something."

He thought for a moment, then asked, "AIDS?"

Nadereh answered seriously, "Maybe not that, but..."

"It's okay. Please believe me. I was not trying to sleep with you."

"I know. You don't have to explain. You should see someone about your problem. You know, your addiction..."

Goodarz's heart sank. "So you asked about me?"

Nadereh was cold and formal, as if she were dealing with someone at work. Without looking at Goodarz, she said, "Of course I've asked about you. It's part of the job. If I hadn't, I wouldn't be here right now treating you like a friend."

Goodarz felt his pulse begin to slow. "So I'm not a stranger to you any longer," he said.

Outside, Goodarz lit a cigarette. It was so cold that their skin tingled as they walked side by side to the shelter.

Nadereh said, "If you have any more cigarettes, I'd like one. When I work nights I don't bring mine with me, so I won't be tempted to smoke. I'm trying to quit."

Goodarz lit a cigarette for Nadereh and said, "If we gave up all our vices, we would be saints."

"Saints or not, that's the way it is. You have to dance to the music they play, or they'll think there's something funny about you and you won't be able to do anything about it."

Goodarz exhaled and said, "Labeled just like me: homeless, a wretch, useless—or a poet, if you wish."

As they walked east along Queen Street, a cold gust of wind swirled around them. They moved faster, trying to get warm. The streetcars and cars were making their way home, but Nadereh and Goodarz were indifferent to the traffic. When Goodarz stopped talking, Nadereh started. After a while their faces, hands, and feet became numb with cold. By the time they reached Nadereh's work place, they felt as if they had been friends forever. After a few nights, Nadereh gave Goodarz her spare key and told him, "I'm working the eleven-to-seven shift this month. You can sleep over at my place, but please make sure you're gone when I get home in the morning. I have to sleep too."

Nadereh's generosity left Goodarz speechless. He was consumed with humility as he gazed into her enormous eyes; her smile made him feel warmer than he'd felt in months. He was so glad to have met a fellow Iranian, even though he could see now that she was not like other Iranian women at all. She could be of mixed descent, maybe with some Indian or African blood, with her beautiful face, dark complexion, and slight build.

Nadereh said, "What's wrong? Why aren't you saying anything? Am I making a mistake?"

He replied, "I'm thinking back to the first time I met you. You really aren't like other Iranians. But I realized at first glance that—"

Nadereh interrupted him. "Yes, at first glance, no one believes I'm Iranian. But I am. Do you have a problem with that? Now answer me. Do you think this is a good suggestion? It makes more sense than coming to the shelter and talking to me all night. Also, some nights I am so busy that I don't have time to talk to you."

"Your offer blows me away. How can you trust me? You don't even know me."

"Don't even mention 'trust.' I've told you my life story. I've got nothing to lose. I don't have any standing in the Iranian community, I don't have any money, and I'm not even a poet or an artist like you. I'm just not important. When someone reaches out for help, I help. I accept people at face value. If they want to be my friend, I welcome them. This offer is only for the time being. You have to find your own place as soon as possible. And remember I told you: you can only stay at night and must be gone during the day."

SOON A MONTH HAD GONE BY, and Goodarz still hadn't found a place. He told her he had saved some money, but Nadereh wouldn't let him leave.

CHAPTER 8

FERDOUS IS SITTING AT A TABLE in the coffee shop in the lobby of St. Michael's hospital, an untouched cup of coffee and a muffin in front of her. People and ideas rotate through her head as quickly as the hospital's revolving door, but still her mind seems cloudy and unfocused. An old man in a wheelchair accompanied by a female orderly sits nearby. A young woman approaches them and says something to the staff member, who pushes the old man in the wheelchair to the entrance and then outside. Samanta and Sasha appear in the hallway with their grandmother. Seeing Ferdous, Samanta runs to her and throws herself into her arms, crying loudly, "Oh, Auntie, Mommy died, Mommy died." She sobs so deeply that her tiny body shakes violently in Ferdous's arms.

Sasha and Grandma stand by quietly, choking back their tears, saying nothing. Ferdous holds Samanta tenderly in her arms, looking over her shoulder at Grandma. Her resemblance to Frida is remarkable—only their age distinguishes mother from daughter. They share the same deep black eyes, but the older woman's are surrounded by deeply carved wrinkles. She has the same small mouth and lips, and her nose is pointed like Frida's. The older woman doesn't speak a single word of English, and Ferdous knows that she wouldn't be able to understand her if Ferdous were to try to express her condolences. Finally, she takes Samanta's face in her hands. She wants to say in English, "I don't believe it." Or, "No, it isn't true." But her command of English fails her at that moment. Instead she says in Farsi, "Oh, *azizam*—"

Suddenly a man approaches them and says something—Ferdous doesn't hear what—and Grandma doesn't let Ferdous finish her condolences. She grabs Samanta's hand, pulls her out of Ferdous's embrace, and follows the man out of the hospital. Ferdous follows them, but they get into a waiting car and are driven away. She waits on the sidewalk until the car turns right at the intersection and disappears from sight.

Samanta's words—"Mommy died, Mommy died"—won't leave Ferdous's head as she walks aimlessly down the street. The little girl's cries match the rhythm of Frida's stride, and Ferdous imagines Frida dancing. In her mind, Ferdous sees Frida being whirled around the dance floor, occasionally spinning so fast that her skirt lifts to show her beautiful legs and allows a glimpse of her panties and lacy slip. She sees Frida proudly wearing her open-collared red dress, her long, thin neck graceful like a swan's. Her small breasts stand out under her dress. Her eyes are two shiny black stones, brilliant and mysterious, and her whole body rhythmically proclaims, "This is me, Frida, the dancer."

The first time she watched Frida dance was at Samanta and Sasha's birthday party. Both she and Ladan had been invited. Ladan was living with her mother at the time, and her company was helping Ferdous to overcome her depression.

Ferdous had heard about Frida from some Iranians she knew. She had been a dancer working in the cheap nightclubs in Madrid when she caught Ghobad's eye. Barely into his twenties, fleeing from the Iran-Iraq war. He was immediately bewitched by Frida's dancing. Money was no problem for Ghobad as his father was a wealthy man in Iran, and he showered Frida and her mother with gifts. He had realized quickly that if he was to gain Frida's love, he had to win over her mother first. He accomplished this with the money that his father sent him for his studies. The mother, too, was wise enough to realize that if her daughter married Ghobad, she would enjoy a far better life than she would if she kept dancing in filthy nightclubs among a bunch of drunks and ne'er do wells. When Ghobad's father found out about Frida, he wasted no time travelling to Madrid to try to prevent his son from marrying her. He had high hopes for his son, but he arrived in Madrid too late—Frida was pregnant. He offered to pay a considerable amount of money to Frida and her mother to get rid of them and the unwanted child, but even after Frida miscarried, Ghobad wouldn't give her up. So his father unhappily arranged a lavish wedding for them and made Frida promise never to dance in public again. He helped them immigrate to Canada and set Ghobad up in a currency exchange office and in an Iranian rug import business. It took Ghobad only a few years to amass considerable wealth, just like his father.

Frida kept her promise to her father-in-law for a few years, but she missed dancing—it had been her whole life from an early age. A mother of twins, she began to dance only at house parties or family events. Ferdous saw her dance a few times; once, when Frida was dancing on a small table, Ferdous had been afraid that she might fall. Ferdous remembered Frida's boast: "I was born to be a dancer and I will die dancing."

When Frida danced, it seemed to Ferdous that she was lost to the world. Dancing transported her to some elevated place where she reigned as a goddess, where nothing and no one could stop her. She was totally in the rhythm of the dance, her eyes fixed on some far-off point, living and breathing perfectly to the music. Her heels and toes beat out a staccato cadence, mesmerizing her audience. Ferdous remembered the first time she had seen Frida dance. During that performance, her daughter had fallen and was hurt, but Frida had been so lost in her dancing that she hadn't even realized her daughter was crying.

Frida's dancing shadow flickering in her mind, Ferdous gets onto a streetcar without thinking, but she gets off after a couple of stops at a place she thinks she's been before. Then she remembers: she is at Nadereh's apartment building. Outside, Mahan is sitting on a bench. She asks, "Did you come to tell Nadereh about Frida's death?"

"To tell her what?"

"Didn't you know?"

"Yes, I knew."

"It was my fault. If I…"

"Why you?"

She stares at Mahan for few seconds and then turns away, not saying anything. All she hears are Frida's shoes, tapping madly to the music in her mind. She runs down the block to the intersection, then turns around and comes back. She thinks she should find Nadereh. Nadereh would assuage her guilt and make her feel better. Nadereh would tell her, "Ghobad should have taken Frida to some other country where he could buy her a kidney. Frida was growing older and sicker each day, becoming a burden. Ghobad might have wanted a younger wife. Ghobad might be just like Ibrahim. Ibrahim got rid of you and then went to Iran and married a twenty-two-year-old."

Ferdous sees Mahan on the other side of the street, walking away. She wants to call out to him and ask him again whether he told Nadereh about Frida's death. But at that moment a truck drives slowly by. When it is gone, Mahan is nowhere to be seen. Inside Nadereh's building, she dials her apartment number, but there's no answer. She keeps on dialing—ten times, twenty times—and still there is no response. Then she remember she's dialing a wrong number. She tries to remember Nadereh's number but she doesn't.

She leaves the building again, and still the tapping of Frida's shoes resonates in her head. Disturbed and confused, she walks the streets and rides public transit aimlessly, switching from one bus to another. Finally, she realizes that she doesn't know what part of the city she is in. The sky is cloudy, and a chilly wind is blowing. She gets on a bus using her last ticket and asks the driver which direction he is going. When Ferdous tells him where she wants to go, he tells her to take another bus going in the opposite direction. When the bus arrives she sits in a seat by the window and lets her thoughts run freely. When the bus reaches the Don Mills and Sheppard intersection, she gets off and enters Fairview Mall. She realizes she hasn't eaten since last night in Parvaneh's place. She is so hungry that she feels nauseated. The sound of Frida's dancing feet is still resonating in her mind.

In the food court, she approaches a counter at random and buys something to eat. But when she takes her first bite, the smell of the greasy meat makes her feel even more queasy. She runs into the washroom to throw up; her whole body is covered in a cold sweat. She washes her face and leaves the washroom, walking aimlessly, window shopping, looking for nothing. She sits on a bench and watches people coming and going. No one notices her. The sound of Frida's feet beat out the message in her mind: *Frida died, Frida died.*

You will be flogged until you tell me where your brother is or you'll be tortured to death.

I didn't tell them, I didn't tell them.

She leaves the mall and walks the streets. Nighttime is coming on, and she watches the city gradually light up. The wind has died down and it is drizzling. She knows this area very well. Finally, she decides to go home. By the time she reaches her building, she is soaking wet. Entering her apartment, she thinks to herself that she hasn't cleaned her place in weeks. She imagines that she can hear her mother scolding her: "My dear, you are so messy...." It is so real.

I didn't betray my brother. I didn't tell them he was hiding behind the bookshelves. I didn't. I didn't.

The answering machine is flickering. She pushes the button and Parvaneh's voice fills the room. "Ferdous, sweetheart, where are you? Why didn't you come up to give your condolences to Frida's children and her mother? I looked for you everywhere. I'll call you...."

She can't hear anything else because the sound of Frida's heels is drowning everything else out.

Zohreh and Nahid, Zohreh and Nahid, they were called at dinner time.
"Lucky them. They're released."
"Released? How do you know that? Perhaps..."
"No, they didn't get released."
"It's not clear. They might be released."
I didn't betray my brother, I didn't tell them.
You will die being flogged if you don't tell us. And if you want to go to paradise, you have to tell us what you know, otherwise.... There's always a palace in paradise for tavabs.

The words from an old song run through her mind the whole night long.

I have a delight in my head
I have a revelation in my heart

The song was only in her head. There was no one else around. It was dawn when the sound of the barrage of bullets filled the ward.

They were released, they were released, they were released.
Mommy died, Mommy died, Mommy died.

She sits by her desk, opens the drawer, and takes out the letter she wrote for Ladan before going to Parvaneh's place. She reads the letter one more time and stares at nothing. Then she tears it up and scatters the pieces on the floor. For a while, she feels as if she has accomplished an important job. She stands still in the middle of room, looking at the pieces of the letter, and then she goes out onto the balcony and leans over the railing. A deep melancholy paralyzes her. It seems as though the end of the world is closing in on her. Soon it will swallow her. The silence of the city is shunning her, as it has from the very beginning, making her want to turn away from her daily sorrows and the failure she has carried within herself for a lifetime. The vast sky invites her to eternity, promising peace and freedom if she leaves behind the life she has lived so far.

I have a delight in my head
I have a revelation in my heart

The streets are empty. The wind is blustery, blowing in all directions, just like Ferdous herself. She feels she is talking to someone who believes her, someone like herself, who tells her, *you are free to go, to go, to go...*

I didn't betray my brother. I didn't, I didn't, I didn't.

MOHAMED, A YOUNG SOMALI MAN returning home from work, finds Ferdous lying on the ground a few metres from her building. Mahan is the first person to be informed of her death.

Ibrahim gives the news to Ferdous's mother, who asks that her body be sent back to Iran for burial in their family mausoleum. Ibrahim is ready to pay, but Ladan won't allow it, arguing that her mother had fled Iran and it was wrong to send her body back there. Finally, Ibrahim gives up and buys a grave beside Frida's. Once in a while, when Frida's mother takes her grandchildren to her daughter's grave, she puts a flower on Ferdous's grave too. Ferdous's grave is rarely visited by anyone else, except Ladan, who comes to her mother's grave just once a year.

CHAPTER 9

WHEN NADEREH AWAKENS, the first thing that catches her eye is the flashing light on her answering machine. The first message is from Parvaneh: "Frida passed away. If you want..."

"I want nothing to do with them," she mumbles. She skips to the next message, but Parvaneh's words are emblazoned on her consciousness. Still, Frida's death can't be real. The message has made her break out in a cold sweat. Struggling to regain her senses, she listens to the next message. It is from Mahan, asking to see her. She can feel her pulse pounding in her throat as she wonders what he could possibly want from her. He hasn't mentioned anything about Frida's death. Maybe that's all it is. The message is brief; already the machine is partway through the next one. It's from someone who calls herself Farah, who wants to get in touch with her regarding her relationship with Ferdous. By the time the last two messages have played, Nadereh is struggling to overcome her shock over Frida's death. She finds herself standing up, grasping onto the bedside chair—she feels dizzy and she can't trust her legs to support her.

Then she notices Goodarz's note. Absorbed in reading it, she ignores the telephone's ring until she hears the same voice on the answering machine, the same one that left the message about Ferdous for her a while ago. Hesitantly, she lifts the receiver to her ear. Farah introduces herself, and then mentions past events that only the two of them could have known. Slowly,

Nadareh begins to remember. Farah. She had been in the Evin prison at the same time as Nadareh. The woman wants to come over, but Nadereh refuses, saying that her roommate might be home.

Farah suggests they meet at the Tim Hortons in the Scarborough Centre. When Nadereh arrives, Farah is waiting. But when Nadereh looks Farah over, she realizes that this woman isn't the person she thought she was. She can't remember if she's even seen her before. This Farah has salt-and-pepper hair gone mostly to white rather than black. She has a dark complexion, with black eyes and a small mouth with narrow lips. She is stout and looks about forty-five years old; but her grey roots indicate that she's older than she appears. She acts motherly toward Nadereh.

"You were with us for a short time," she says, "but I remember you very well. Your belly was huge when they released you—that's what I remember the most. You were very young and naive, and you kept asking everyone about your husband. When you heard he'd been killed in a street fight, you couldn't believe it. Some women, the *tavabs*, I mean, made fun of you. So tell me, since you've been released, where have you been and what happened to make you come to Canada?"

Nadereh is still trying to place her. When had she met the woman who is sitting in front of her, staring at her with her compassionate eyes and talking to her in a Turkish accent? Goodarz's note, the events of the previous night at Parvaneh's, the sudden death of Frida, and Mahan's mysterious request keep playing over and over in her mind. Harshly, she asks the woman, "Have you dragged me out here to investigate me? If you're an immigration officer, I am pleased to inform you that I've got my citizenship and I've had it for years now."

Farah laughs loudly and says, "I've nothing to do with your citizenship. To tell you the truth, since I've heard the rumours…" She pauses for a moment and then continues. "I've only been here a few months myself."

Nadereh is still angry. She asks, "Are you looking for a case for your refugee claim?"

Farah says softly, "No, let me finish. Back then you—"

"Forget about 'back then,'" Nadereh says crossly.

She looks around. People of all nationalities, mostly immigrant families, are spending their Sunday window shopping and looking for bargains in the mall. Nadereh stares at them, oblivious to where she is; she is consumed with her thoughts. Suddenly, she remembers Farah's message on the answering machine and says, "You told me you wanted to talk about Ferdous."

"Yes, Ferdous is the reason that I wanted to see you. I heard that you and Parvaneh..."

Nadereh wants to ask her how she knows Parvaneh, but she refrains. All she really wants is to get rid of Farah. She doesn't know her; she has no memory of her. She hasn't had time yet to think about the other events: Frida's death, Goodarz's leaving. His reason isn't clear and she doesn't know what part she played in his decision. Now that Frida is dead, she is overcome with guilt about trying to prevent Ferdous from donating her kidney. It is as though her conscience is telling her, *if you hadn't tried to stop Ferdous, Frida would still be alive.*

Farah asks, "Are you listening to me?"

Letting go of her thoughts, Nadereh asks, "How do you know Parvaneh?"

Farah says, "I haven't met her, but she is well known in the Iranian community. However," she continues, "you shouldn't feel sorry for Ferdous. She's responsible for the deaths of more than one person. She betrayed her own brother. She was a *tavab.* Did you know that?"

"So what? Many prisoners were *tavabs.*"

"This one is different from the others. She's responsible for their deaths."

Nadereh says nothing. She feels like she is disoriented, falling. She remembers how sorry she felt for Ferdous and how much she has done to help her. Then she thinks of Frida. She says, "Maybe it's a good thing, then, that Frida died before she could get Ferdous's kidney."

"Frida died? When?"

"Last night."

Nadereh sits staring at Farah, who continues in a kind, motherly tone, "I know all about Ferdous. I only found out you were here in Canada because word got around that you were helping her. I told myself that maybe you didn't know anything about Ferdous's past. Please don't do it anymore. If I were you, I wouldn't even talk to her. Stop being her friend. These kinds of people aren't worth a cent."

"I thought she'd been a victim. How stupid and foolish I was. I wish I could talk about it with Parvaneh."

Remembering Parvaneh and Mahan, she suddenly feels uneasy.

Farah says, "Parvaneh knows about her. I wonder why she hasn't told you anything."

Nadereh watches people strolling around, trying to digest everything that has happened. After a while, her mind drifts back to the conversation she'd had with Parvaneh, when Parvaneh had said, "I want to tell you something, but it's a secret."

"What?" Nadereh had asked.

Parvaneh had turned away from the window, looked at Nadereh, and then said, "I don't know for sure if it's true or not, but rumour has it that Ferdous was a prisoner, even though she denies it."

Nadereh stared at Parvaneh and said, "Well, is it a sin to be a prisoner? I was a prisoner too."

"She was a *tavab*."

"What kind of *tavab*? There were many of them. Some were forced to be. Otherwise..."

"I don't know how. I don't know anything else about her past. She's no different from anyone else to me. She's a miserable person who needs help. You can help her. She has nobody. Her husband abandoned her. From what I heard, he used her as a way to get into Canada. He came here on Ferdous's money, but she still loves and admires him. Whatever else she has done is none of my business. All I know is that she's a deeply depressed woman."

"How do you know all this?"

Parvaneh answered, "I am a social worker. Haven't you told me everything about your past too?"

"What can I do for her?"

"Help her. She's a broken woman. Her husband has taken her daughter away. She splits her time between the psychiatric hospital and her apartment. Her mother is supposed to arrive one of these days. Help her. Forget about whatever she might have done before; it's her business."

"So Parvaneh never told you anything?" Farah says. Then she asks herself, "Why not?"

"I don't know. She mentioned something, but she didn't go into detail. She said, Ferdous had been a *tavab*. Then..."

"Ohhh, I get it. Parvaneh isn't supposed to talk about anyone's past. She's a social worker."

Nadereh sets her coffee on the table and looks at Farah suspiciously. *Am I dreaming*, she wonders. Since last night, everything has become fuzzy and unreal. Doubtfully, she says, "How do I know that you're telling me the truth? Parvaneh won't believe me."

"I'm telling you—a lot of people know about Ferdous. I'm wondering why no one else has told you about her already."

Nadereh is confused. "Why?" she asks Farah, and then stops talking. It is as though she's asking herself.

She remembers taking Ferdous to a cultural program at the North York library. It took quite a bit of coaxing to convince Ferdous to come with her. "Come on, you're always stuck at home," Nadereh had said. "What's wrong with you? Why are you keeping yourself away from people?"

During the break, she ran into her friend Hamideh, whom

Parvaneh had introduced her to. They sometimes saw each other at these kinds of events or met casually when they were out in the Iranian community. She'd heard from Parvaneh that Hamideh had been behind bars in Evin for a few years too.

Ferdous, as usual, was standing in a corner, not making any effort to mingle. When Hamideh had spotted Nadereh with Ferdous, she'd pulled Nadereh's sleeve and led her away to a corner, asking, "How do you know that skinny woman?"

"What do you mean, how do I know that—"

Before Nadereh finished, Hamideh spoke up. "Didn't you know that she was a *tavab*?"

Still angry, Nadereh answered, "It's none of your business. How do I know whether or not you are—"

Hamideh stopped her and said softly, "I'm concerned for you. Otherwise—"

Nadereh didn't stay to hear the rest. She looked for Ferdous but couldn't find her. Abruptly, she'd left the library.

Nadereh stands up and faces Farah. She tries to remember who she really is. Farah's grey hair and complexion make her look sick and old. Her face is bony and her cheeks are sunken, but her black eyes still shine with maternal kindness.

But last night's anger and disillusionment have only gotten worse. Nadereh says, "You're just messing with my head."

Farah ponders this for a moment, then replies, "Why is Ferdous's life so important to you? She's the daughter of a rich *haji* who betrayed her close friends and sold out her own brother as soon as things got tough in prison."

"Why didn't you tell me earlier?"

Gently, Farah replies, "Yes, I should have told you earlier. To tell you the truth, I wasn't even aware that you were here. Then I heard your name by chance while I was talking with some friends about Frida's kidney transplant. A lot of Iranians know about it. Maybe Ferdous started telling everyone herself so she'd look better; perhaps she wanted people to forget that she was once a *tavab*."

Nadereh says, "I'm going to throw up." She rushes to the washroom. She feels like she wants to be sick, but she can't; instead, her stomach just keeps on churning. Farah stands beside her and massages her shoulders. Nadereh washes her face. Farah hands her a paper towel to dry her face, and they leave the washroom. Then Farah asks, "What are you going to do?"

"What should I do?" Then she remembers Goodarz. *Maybe he can help,* she thinks.

Staring at Farah, she says, "I'm going to leave the city, maybe today or tomorrow. There's nothing here for me anymore."

"Why should you leave? Ferdous should be the one to leave."

When they reach the mall exit, Nadereh turns to say goodbye. Farah asks, "When can I see you again?"

"I told you, I'm leaving."

She walks a few steps, then returns and puts her hand on Farah's shoulder. "What's the matter?" Farah asks.

"What about Ibrahim, Ferdous's ex-husband?" Nadereh asks. "Was he a *tavab* too? Was he a political prisoner?"

"I don't know. I didn't know him."

Nadereh concludes that he probably wasn't able to put up with Ferdous.

When Nadereh turns to leave, Farah says, "Are you really going to leave Toronto? Have you found a job somewhere else, or are you going somewhere for a holiday?"

Nadereh doesn't answer. She doesn't know what she will do. She only knows that, because of what she now knows, she doesn't have the strength to face Mahan and Parvaneh. A sadness has gripped her heart that she can't share with anyone. She should leave. Maybe leaving would be punishment enough for her foolishness. She hates herself for being so gullible.

When she arrives home, she phones the shelter to ask for an emergency leave. She needs the week off. She calls a friend, planning to give her the key to her apartment, but she changes her mind. She isn't able to wait for her friend to come and get the key.

"Forget about it," she says. "I'll be back in a week."

But when she gets on a bus for Vancouver, she's sure that she won't come back to Toronto. She asks herself, *why Vancouver?* It seems as if somebody is telling her to find Goodarz. He had always said, *"If I had to leave this city, I'd go to Vancouver, to the shores of the Pacific Ocean."*

In her mind, she imagines she is talking to Goodarz: "You're not the only one who killed someone. I did too."

CHAPTER 10

THE WEATHER IS OPPRESSIVELY GLOOMY, more than just a rainy day. Heavy, dark clouds on the horizon blend into the ocean to the point where there is no distinction between water and sky. The tall buildings on the waterfront seem to be looming up right out of the ocean. Nadereh watches a flock of gulls flying over the harbour and imagines herself to be just a tiny spot amid the splendour. At times, she is overwhelmed by the beauty of her new home. Her need for Goodarz grows into a bold desire. She imagines him with her, working on expressing himself through his poetry. She would beg him to write it down, and he would answer, "When I want to write it down, it flies away."

The beauty of the vista before her reminds her of a few of the poems that Goodarz had recited, but she can only remember bits and pieces of them. This vast, indescribable magnificence surrounding her is so breathtaking that she sometimes thinks it must be an illusion.

Absorbed in her own thoughts, she hardly notices the chilling cold that passes through her clothing and penetrates her bones. Holding the handle of Ehsan's stroller, she pushes it along slowly. He is nine years old, but developmentally he is still very much at the toddler stage. She can see an inexpressible sadness and sometimes an enormous joy in his big brown eyes. He always has a smile on his face and he's always affectionate and loving with his mother, his full-time caregiver. Even after all these years, Nadereh fails to understand the noises that he produces in his efforts to communicate. When he is restless and Nadereh can't calm him, she imagines he is asking for the father he lost three years ago. When Goodarz was still around, he had been the one who mostly took care of their son.

The ocean is asleep under the heavy clouds, and nothing can disturb its deep serenity. Tiny waves lap upon the shore in a melancholy rhythm, like a mother's lamentation for her long-lost son, for whom she still grieves. They are in Stanley Park, and fewer people than usual are out: only a few young people jogging or skateboarding, some older couples out for their daily walk, and a few new mothers and babies.

In front of a huge rock at the edge of the ocean is a sheltered bench where Nadereh usually sits to rest and feed Ehsan. To get there, she pushes Ehsan's stroller, watching the ocean and the gulls, and envying their freedom. She talks to her son, practising the exercises they've given her at the speech therapy centre. She's not sure how much he learns at school. She hopes that one day she will be able to communicate with him. The doctor also told her that, if he practises every day, Ehsan might be able to walk with crutches eventually. They can do the physiotherapy outdoors when the weather is fine. For Nadereh, the exercises are essential—a commitment, a duty—and she makes them part of her daily routine. To her, the park beside the ocean is a second home and the birds are friends and acquaintances; they fly overhead watching and sympathizing with her. She is more familiar with nature than with people. If it is raining, she has to stay home—where she finds it hard to perform the physiotherapy and speech-therapy exercises with Ehsan—or take him to a mall, which she doesn't like either. She becomes bored easily and yells at the boy if he gets fretful. Then she regrets her bad behaviour and kisses him and cries over him to make up.

Three years after Goodarz left, Nadereh still can't set aside the pain of the loss. He was like a saviour, helping her bury her old, deep wounds from her past. She still loved Mahan, however, even while she was living with Goodarz. Goodarz knew, even though he never mentioned it and she didn't talk to him about it. Whenever Nadereh dreamed of Mahan, which happened frequently, Goodarz could always tell, because she was always melancholy and sad the next day. One day when Nadereh woke up to Ehsan's cry, Goodarz wasn't there. He'd left a brief note and disappeared from her life again. After he was gone, it was as if a new side of him suddenly appeared to her—now, the man resembled a saint—and Nadereh tormented herself with feelings of anger and guilt, realizing she had come to know the real Goodarz too late. Now her chance was gone, and she had no hope that Goodarz would come back. She felt guilty for not showing any love or even appreciation for him—he had taken care of Ehsan full-time so that she could attend university. She had lived with him as if she had had no other choice. After he disappeared, she realized that she had pushed him away. She had needed to make herself busy enough so that she wouldn't have time think about her own life.

After Goodarz's disappearance, Ehsan's disability became her punishment, one that she would bear forever, and Mahan slowly faded from her memory. Sometimes when she was tired of her life and her ordeals, it crossed her mind to institutionalize her child and leave for another part of the world, as Goodarz had. But the boy's huge, brown eyes, which looked so much like her own, suggested that he knew what was going on in her mind. He would look at his mother with such a sad and curious expression on her face that she couldn't stand it and she would start to cry. Hugging him and crying loudly, she would say, "No, I will never leave you, my baby." And so it goes—day after day, year after year.

When she reaches her bench, a man is sitting on it. His profile seems familiar, but it doesn't occur to her that he might be an acquaintance. He doesn't seem to notice her approach; he sits as still as a statue, absorbed in watching the horizon.

Nadereh parks the stroller and wipes a corner of the bench with a piece of cloth. When she sits down, the man turns and looks at her. For a few moments, she feels like she's in a dream, an old dream that she'd struggled to forget. She's speechless, and it seems like the man is as well. They stare at each other, spellbound, neither believing who or what they are seeing. Ehsan starts to make his incomprehensible sounds, breaking the spell. Nadereh recovers herself, but Mahan still sits transfixed, watching her; it is clear that she cares about her child. When Nadereh finishes soothing the boy, she turns to Mahan and gazes into his face, which seems to have aged more than twenty years. Neither utters a word. Finally, Nadereh collects herself and asks, "What brings you here?" Her question is ironic and teasing, as if no time has passed. Then she adds, "Maybe you're here for a vacation!"

When she notices the profound sadness in Mahan's eyes, she instantly regrets having spoken to him so flippantly. She remembers Parvaneh and Mahasti and asks him seriously, "How are your wife and daughter? Mahasti must be a beautiful young woman by now." She won't allow herself to say Parvaneh's name. Before Mahan can answer, her son needs her attention again. She quiets Ehsan, then turns back to Mahan and stares at him. The man has changed. It isn't only the years and early old age that have changed him; there is a shadow in his face, a thoughtfulness that wasn't there before. She can't bear to look at him any longer, and she turns away, but not before seeing the tears welling up in his eyes and beginning to flow down his cheeks. Her sarcasm dies within her.

Perplexed, she asks, "Why are you crying?" Mahan tries to wipe away his tears with the tips of his fingers, but it's no use. For a moment, there is silence between them. *Has Parvaneh died?* Nadereh wonders. Mahan has taken his eyes from her and is watching the ocean again. Nadereh thinks about Parvaneh, wondering what could have happened. Not sure whether she has asked or not, she inquires again, "How's your wife?"

Had she mentioned Mahasti? She's not sure, so she continues, "And Mahasti?"

Mahan takes his eyes from the ocean and looks at Nadereh. This time there's pride in his eyes. With a trembling voice he says, "Mahasti left us."

Nadereh feels the ground fall away beneath her feet. It's as if she is suspended in some awful place. A question dances in her mind: *Is she dead?* She tries to recover her composure and asks, "What do you mean?"

Despite his deep sorrow, Mahan smiles, and he says, "She left us to devote her life to the poor, but I believe she also wanted to punish us. It's been three years, and we haven't had any news from her...."

Nadereh fights to regain her composure and then she gently places her hand on Mahan's arm. His light brown eyes, which age has surrounded with wrinkles, are red and full of tears. Nadereh is speechless. She wants to say, "*Young people sometimes...*" but the words don't come. She stares into Mahan's eyes, and searches for the Mahan she remembers from years ago.

She asks herself what good could possibly come from rehashing her reasons for leaving. *We could have been together.... No, it's better this way....*

Mahan says, "Do you remember that night when you and Goodarz came to our house with Ferdous? After you left, Parvaneh and I had a big fight. She blamed you for everything, and I couldn't stand it."

Nadereh says, "Yes, I remember.... I left Toronto the next day. Actually, it was because I had heard something about Ferdous. I felt that it would be better for all of us if I stepped out of your life."

She wants to add that she had also been thinking about what was best for Mahasti, but bites her tongue.

Mahan asks, "Why did you run?"

She sits back. Her voice becomes serious. "To tell you the truth, I was tired of the way things were going. I thought I should get away for a while and think about my life, but I couldn't bring myself to come back and arrange for the things I'd left behind. I asked one of my friends to do it for me. I knew that I didn't belong in your life. I was becoming a burden, a..." She trails off.

Mahan stares at her. "When you suddenly disappeared, my life started to fall apart. It felt like I wasn't myself anymore. Parvaneh saw it too. It was beyond my control. Everything became shallow and meaningless: my family, my wife, my child, my work, the community, everything. Then my life completely fell apart. I didn't care about my family and my home anymore. I kept going to work, but at home.... How can I explain it? It felt like I was just acting out a part. Sometimes I really hated my role. Once, I left home and didn't come back for a couple of days. Parvaneh was so mad at me. In spite of all of this, she tried her best to keep our family from falling apart, but it was impossible."

He stops talking. Nadereh puts her hand on his arm and says, "Forgive me. I didn't want to wreck your life. I thought it would be better if I left. I ran because I wanted you and Mahasti—"

Mahan interrupts her. "No, no. I could never blame you. Whatever happened, it was all my own fault. My marriage with Parvaneh.... I always blame myself for the day you came to the hospital with your dead baby in your arms and left without him. I should—"

Ehsan starts to fuss again, saying his only word: "Baba." Nadereh gets up and turns his stroller around so that he is facing them. Holding on to her son's hand, she says, "That's better; he can see us this way. Whenever I talk to someone else, it bothers him. I think he feels jealous, or he's afraid of losing me. How can I reassure him? The little guy still can't talk. He calls me Baba."

Mahan asks, "Is he your son?"

"Yes, he is my son, and Goodarz's son."

A look of understanding comes into Mahan's eyes. He says,

"I'm sorry. All I've been doing is talking about myself. What about you? I heard that you moved to Vancouver and married Goodarz. To tell you the truth, I followed you, a few months after you left. I had tried to make myself forget you but I couldn't. I had feelings for you; whether it was love or not, I don't know. Since the first time I met you in the hospital, I had a feeling about you. I really didn't know if it was regret or love. Living with Parvaneh was like a departure from my real life.

"When you reappeared, I didn't want to force myself to accept the fact that I loved you. And then we all went camping together. You remember the trip, don't you? I was wrestling with myself then to make a decision. I couldn't understand what was wrong with me. Maybe Mahasti was a factor, too. It was impossible to decide, and it was getting harder and harder to keep on pretending.

"Then, when I found out you had married Goodarz, I went back to Toronto and continued with Parvaneh. But it was a disaster! Parvaneh saw right through me; she knew that I wasn't the same person. It was out of my control. I isolated myself for months; I didn't talk to anyone. I would leave home for three or four days at a time. It was after one of my absences that I came home to find that Mahasti had disappeared. She hadn't finished high school yet, and it took a few months before we found out that she had volunteered to work with children in Ghana. She wrote and asked us to leave her alone. In her brief letter, she said that while most of world's population was struggling to find a piece of bread to survive, we were haunted by our personal and trivial problems. At the beginning, Parvaneh believed that she would come home, that it was a teenage thing that would pass. But it's been three years already. She not only hasn't come back, but she has never written us again. Every once in a while, we search her name on Google to find out where she is. But we don't have an address or email for her. So, that's it. She's disappeared from our lives."

As abruptly as he began, Mahan stops talking. Tears run down his cheeks.

Nadereh looks into Mahan's eyes with compassion and says, "You should be proud of your daughter. Nowadays, you can't find many young people like her. Most of them care just about themselves. The best ones are those who travel and explore the world. The rest just get a degree if they can and find a job—they don't care what's going on in the world. Mahasti is a special young woman."

Having regained his composure, Mahan says quietly, "Yes, you're right. But as a father, I still can't believe what happened. After Mahasti's disappearance, Parvaneh and I were constantly fighting; she blamed herself and I insisted that she was wrong, that it was all my fault."

Ehsan starts crying again, and Nadereh gets up to look after him. "Sorry, I have to take care of my baby." Lovingly, she hugs Ehsan and pats his back, then bends over to calm him down, kissing him and murmuring to him. She takes a banana from her bag on the back of the stroller; she peels it and breaks it into little pieces and puts them on a paper plate in front of Ehsan, who bats it away with the back of his hand. Nadereh kisses him again and consoles him lovingly, then she turns to Mahan. "I don't know why he's so upset. It's better if we walk. He might fall asleep; he seems tired."

They walk side by side for a while. Nadereh turns and looks at Mahan, who is gazing out over the ocean. He has the same taciturn expression she knew from years ago. She remembers Mahasti with her long, straight hair falling down to her shoulders, and her big brown eyes that were so much like her father's, always dressed in colourful shirts and jeans. She had called her Auntie Nadereh. When she was younger, whenever Nadereh would go to visit, Mahasti would run to her and say, "Auntie Nadereh, will you read me the Paria poem?" Nadereh would sit her on her lap and read her the poem from her book.

Now, Mahasti is like a question mark in her mind. She wonders how that spoiled little girl could have become so rebellious as to leave her parents. Mahasti was almost ten when Nadereh left Toronto, but she had seemed much younger because of her tiny body and her doting parents. She remembers how Mahan would wrap her in his arms like a five-year-old and tenderly kiss her forehead.

She wants to continue talking about what has happened. "It was my fault. That night, I shouldn't…" Suddenly she remembers Ferdous and says, "The next day, a woman called me and said she knew something about Ferdous. So we arranged to meet and she told me things about Ferdous that made me hate myself for trusting her. Actually, that was partly why I decided I couldn't stay in Toronto any longer. I couldn't bring myself to believe that I had been helping a person whose hands were so stained with other people's blood. I didn't have any problems with her being a *tavab*. I knew it wasn't easy to be tortured and still remain strong and faithful to the cause. Anybody could break down and betray someone, but to bring about someone's death…"

Mahan is off in his own world and doesn't seem to follow what Nadereh is saying. She continues, "If Ferdous had been executed…" She stops talking, then after a few moments adds, "I'm talking nonsense. If Ferdous had been the one who left, there wouldn't have been any problem. To tell you the truth, I wasn't sure why I ran away. Goodarz left the same day. He had left me, and suddenly I felt lonely and I panicked. Goodarz could have helped me face the situation. Actually, I wasn't planning to leave forever, but when I came to Vancouver and found Goodarz, I decided to stay here and remove myself from your life. Honestly, everything came apart that night."

She looks at Mahan and continues, "And I didn't want to…" She couldn't continue.

Mahan says, "I know. You don't need to explain. You were honest with yourself. But me, I don't know."

Without waiting for Mahan's to continue, she says, "The most important thing was that I lost my trust in people. I wasn't myself anymore."

They share a few moments of silence, neither one daring to ask the other any more questions. The things she had learned about Ferdous came back to her. After she had left Toronto, she had made an effort to forget everything about Ferdous. Thinking about all she had done to help her left her feeling sad and angry with herself for allowing herself to be fooled. Whenever Goodarz mentioned how badly Ferdous had misled her, she refused to think about it or allow herself to be angry with him. Had he maybe heard something, too? Not likely. If he had, he definitely would have said something. He was uncanny when it came to reading people. Wasn't he the one who had realized her love for Mahan? Also, he had told her many times, *don't get mixed up with these people. There's a huge gulf between you and them. Leave them alone.* But she didn't understand him until it was too late.

Collecting herself, she blurts out, "What happened to Ferdous? I really want to know what she did after Frida's death. She thought that if she donated her kidney, everyone would forget about what she had done in her past."

Mahan looks at Nadereh, surprised. "Didn't you know? It was in all of the Iranian papers. Ferdous killed herself the same day Frida died. She jumped off her balcony. Her body lay in the street for hours until someone found her."

Nadereh stops walking and stares at Mahan, totally astounded. The shocked look in Nadereh's eyes unsettles Mahan. "I thought you knew. All the newspapers wrote about it."

"Newspapers?"

"Yes, all the Iranian newspapers."

"Back then, I wasn't sure where I was or where I was going. I wasn't even aware of my surroundings. The only thing I knew for sure was that I left for Vancouver on the same day that Frida died."

Mahan puts his hand on Nadereh's shoulder and hesitantly said, "I wanted to know: have you been happy?"

Somehow, Ehsan manages to turn himself around in his stroller. He reaches out for his mother, crying again. She keeps on pushing the stroller, ignoring his restlessness. She still hasn't answered Mahan. *What good would it do to answer anyway?*

When she looks back on everything, she can see that these pitiful melodramas, including her own sad life, are all hopelessly intertwined. *Would there never be any happiness for any of them?* Blocking out the black thoughts, she returns to her old tough self and asks with a trace of irony in her voice, "How's Parvaneh? Is she happy with her work?"

Mahan turns back to her. In his clinical voice, he replies, "Parvaneh? She lives and breathes her work; she's totally consumed by it. She's managed to ease the pain of Mahasti's disappearance. In a way she's proud of her, boasting about her in public, but I can say for sure that she misses her terribly. She is burying herself in her work. She took some university courses, and now she works in a centre for children with disabilities. I admire her independence. She's very strong. Just putting up with me proves how strong she is."

Nadereh pauses for a few moments, considering her response. Finally, she looks at Mahan and says, "Fortunately or unfortunately, the world has been built by these kinds of people, people who can get along in any situation. I never really got to know Parvaneh. Sometimes she was more than nice and sometimes she was narrow-minded and selfish. But I can't say that she ever wronged me. She helped me go to school, find a job, and stand on my feet. I didn't do any harm to her, either. I was truthful and honest with her. I was honest with everybody."

She just keeps on walking and pushing the stroller. Without looking at Mahan she says, "Goodarz loved me deeply. I mean, he really was in love with me, without expecting anything in return. But I didn't appreciate him until after he left."

Reaching down to pat Ehsan's shoulder, she continues, "This is the fruit of our love, a disabled boy. Now Goodarz is gone and all I've got is Ehsan. Maybe this is the punishment I'll always have to endure because of my ingratitude. You know, I've never really believed in this type of thing, and I still don't, but sometimes I think life has its own cruel way of making things right."

She stops talking for a few moments, thinking, then continues. "Sometimes I think I shouldn't blame myself. After Ehsan was born, and after Goodarz found out that there wasn't any hope for him to get well, he sometimes sugggested that it would be better to place him in an institution and for us go away, to explore the world. But I couldn't do it."

"So he left you?"

"Yes, he left me. The note he left said that he wasn't willing to take care of a child with disabilities for the rest of his life."

"When? When did it happen?"

"Three years ago.

"And you've lived alone for the past three years?"

"Not exactly alone—with my son. I named him Ehsan, in memory of the first man in my life; the man who lost his life to his dreams."

"My God, Nadereh, you've had a hard life. Why didn't you tell me? If I'd only known... What happened to your son?"

Finally able to share the story of her burden, Nadereh relaxes, feeling the words flow easily from her mouth. She has never told anyone the full story before. Even when she speaks to social workers, she tells them only the things that can be written in files, leaving out anything that might elicit their sympathy. Serenely, she says, "I don't know. Sometimes I blame it on the sperm of an addict.... But Goodarz had quit the drugs a long time ago. I did too—I quit smoking when I found out I was pregnant. One of the doctors told me it happened during childbirth. I was in labour for a long time. They didn't want to give me a C-section. They thought that because my first baby had been born through natural childbirth, I could have this one naturally too. But, when I couldn't push him out, they tried to use forceps, but that didn't work either. So they took me to into another room, where they used a vacuum device to deliver him. The doctor told me that the baby didn't receive enough oxygen and that the delay caused by moving me resulted in brain damage. Of course, some of the other doctors didn't agree and blamed Goodarz and me because we were smokers before getting pregnant. Later on, I found out that if they had admitted they were at fault, I would have been able to sue them."

"Why didn't you do that?"

"What good would it have done? It wouldn't give me back my child's health. Anyway, I didn't find out that I could have sued the hospital until Goodarz was gone. Who has the patience to put up with the courts, the lawyers, the bureaucracy? Ehsan needed me to take care of him, and that was my priority. It still is."

The sky starts to clear. Some patches of blue start to appear. A flock of gulls flies over, screeching as if they are happy to see the weather clearing.

Nadereh breaks the silence. Something has burst deep inside her; all her bad experiences are draining from her soul, as these previously unspoken words come pouring out. "Sometimes I think my disabled child is the fruit of a grand dream that our fathers and our generation hatched. My first husband, Ehsan, like many others, lost his life for those dreams. Sometimes I just think that there's no fairness in life."

Nadereh's words remind Mahan of Mahasti's disappearance. "Maybe," he suggests, "losing Mahasti is a result of these dreams too."

Nadereh looks at Mahan and says, "If your daughter is devoting her life to helping the poor, you should be proud of her. You shouldn't blame yourself. She's an exceptional person."

They reach the end of the shoreline, and Nadereh turns toward her street. She thinks about Ferdous again. "I was always afraid that Ferdous might kill herself. I always looked at her as a victim. But in the end, she had me fooled too. I didn't know how deep her problems ran. I knew she felt bad for what she had done and that she had asked for forgiveness, but I didn't know that she had betrayed people. She even didn't blame Ibrahim when he abandoned her."

"What was wrong with her?"

Nadereh shrugs her shoulders and waves her hands, as though she is dismissing the thought. "Forget about it. Why waste our breath? Actually, she poisoned my life. When I found out what she had done, I was disgusted with myself and with her. But now when I look back, I think we were both victims.

They leave the shore behind, and Nadereh pushes Ehsan's stroller onto a street lined on both sides with houses and tall buildings. Before long, she stops in front of one of the high-rises. Looking up, Mahan can see that most of the balconies are decorated with plants and flower boxes. She says, "This is where I live. I guess I should take Ehsan home."

She holds out her hand for Mahan to shake. He implores, "Won't you invite me in for a cup of tea?"

Nadereh's eyes take on a faraway look. "Sorry, I really have to say no. By the time I get this little guy settled, I won't have enough energy left to entertain any guests. He needs a new diaper—I know he is wet—then I have feed him his lunch and put him to bed. I also have to finish a paper before noon tomorrow."

She puts out her hand again, and Mahan takes it in his. He pulls her toward him and suddenly they hug each other, staying clasped for a while. But then Nadereh pulls herself out of Mahan's arms and starts toward her building. Startled, he says, "Tonight I'm going back to Toronto. I'm here for a one-day conference. I'm planning to go back to Iran soon. My father has written to tell me he's sick, and I want to see him before something happens to him. I might stay there. I came to Canada to raise my daughter, but I never expected to lose her here." His voice breaking, he continues. "Actually, her leaving was like a lesson to me. It showed me that I'm wasting my time here...."

Ehsan is crying loudly, and Nadereh can't hear the rest of Mahan's words. She says, simply, "Goodbye." There is something in her voice that causes Mahan to mouth goodbye under his breath as he turns away. After a few steps, he stops and turns back toward Nadereh, who is standing by the building, watching him. He isn't the same Mahan of years ago, but she isn't the same person either. She says, "I wish you good luck, going back home." Then she opens the big glass door of the building and pushes Ehsan inside. The boy stops crying.

A LITTLE MORE THAN A YEAR AFTER Mahan's visit, Nadereh receives a letter from the city of Saary in Iran. Mahan Daavar's name is written in English on the top left corner of the envelope. Excitedly, she tears open the letter and quickly pores over it. When she reaches the last sentence, she goes back to the beginning to read it again and again, at least ten times. It is long—four pages—and it asks her to visit him in Iran with her son. He also confesses his love for her. He tells her that he has loved her from the first time he set eyes on her in the hospital in Iran. He says that he has never been able to forget her innocent, childlike eyes asking for help. He assures her that she won't regret travelling to Iran, and he makes it clear that, if she wants to, she can go back to Canada whenever she wants. He offers to pay the cost of the trip for her and Ehsan. He is certain that if she comes to Iran, she'd soon forget about returning to Canada. Finally, he tells her that his parents' estate included his childhood home, which he plans to turn into a rehabilitation centre for disabled children. He hopes to build a three-bedroom home on the property for himself and, he hopes, for her and Ehsan. He has hired staff, including a young doctor and two nurses.

Each time Nadereh gets to the end of the letter, she declares loudly and enthusiastically, "He loves me. After so many years, he still loves me!" She hugs Ehsan and kisses him again and again as she shouts, "He loves me, he loves me. He's always been in love with me!"

She is so thrilled about the possibility of a new destiny that she finds it hard to sleep that night. The next day when she wakes up, she wonders if it was just a dream. She reads the letter again, but this time thoughts of Parvaneh and Mahasti intrude on her joy and she can't quite block out a feeling of guilt. She can't seem to shake their images from her mind.

When Ehsan wakes up, she receives yet another happy surprise. For the first time ever, he calls her "Ma." Joyfully, she hugs and kisses him, saying, "Yes, I'm your mother, your mommy."

As the day goes by, her emotions rise and fall, but she can't quite overcome her elation over Mahan's confession. Still, her sense of honour compels her to write to Parvaneh. Somehow, this decision eases the feeling of deep sadness that she has carried with her for her whole life. As she starts to write the letter, her memories of the happy moments she had shared with the three of them come flooding back.

Ever since she left Toronto, she has barely given any thought to the life she lived there; she's tried not to remember anything. Even when Goodarz was with her, whenever she was reminded of their old life, she would push the memory away. Mahan's letter has revived her memories, especially the happy ones. She thinks about when she'd just arrived in Toronto and had stayed at Parvaneh's, and she remembers the day that Mahan had talked about that young woman with her dead child. How clever she had been not to tell him she was that same woman. If Parvaneh had known, she might have discovered Mahan's feelings toward her and sent her away. She might even have believed that Nadereh had come to Canada to get closer to Mahan. How wise Nadereh had been to hide her love for Mahan.

She remembers Ehsan, her first love, who had faded from her mind after so many years. *"We shouldn't take food from the mouths of those less fortunate."* When and where had she heard Ehsan say that? She can't remember, but she's sure it was him she'd heard it from. She thinks about whether Ehsan's philosophy should stop her from going to Mahan and taking him from Parvaneh, even though Mahan has begged her to come.

She keeps her letter to Parvaneh short and straightforward. She begins by thanking Parvaneh for all her help, encouraging her to continue her education, which Nadereh herself had always been prevented from doing. She tells Parvaneh that, even after so many years, she still feels indebted to her. She finishes the letter by telling her that she had met Mahan accidentally when he'd travelled to Vancouver for a conference. At the end of their short visit, Mahan had told her that he was going back to Iran, probably forever. He had been very lonely and depressed. Finally, she encourages Parvaneh to go to her husband and stay with him. She rewrites the letter several times until she is happy with it. *Go back to your husband and your country and say good-bye to exile*, she repeats. She puts the letter in an envelope as soon as she is finished and mails it the same day, before she can change her mind.

Leaving the post office, she doesn't go home, even though it is four in the afternoon and the day nearing its end. She pushes Ehsan to Stanley Park and sits on the same bench where she sat with Mahan. It's a sunny day. The grandness of the ocean reflects her sense of serenity and joy.

She looks back on her memories of Mahan. His love is a refuge in the cruel world. Every once in a while, she kisses Ehsan and says to him, "He still loves me, and that's enough for me." She never answers Mahan's letter, and he never writes to her again.

ABOUT A YEAR LATER she receives a letter from Parvaneh, thanking her for her wise and compassionate advice; it has come from the same address as Mahan's letter. Inside the envelope is a photo of Parvaneh and Mahan. A baby girl sits on Parvaneh's lap, and another girl, who looks about six or seven, stands next to Mahan. On the wall behind them a portrait of a young woman, her hair tied at the back of her head, looks strikingly like Mahasti.

She slowly opens the letter and sees Parvaneh's familiar handwriting. Parvaneh tells Nadereh that she is indebted to her for her new life. She explains that she and Mahan had adopted the older girl in Canada. They named her Bahar, an Iranian name that corresponds with her original name, April. The little girl sitting on Parvaneh's lap was abandoned as a newborn and left at their door. They adopted her and named her Rayhaneh in memory of Nadereh's little sister, who was killed in the war. Parvaneh also mentions that Mahasti will be coming to visit them in the near future. At the end of the letter, Parvaneh invites Nadereh and her son to Iran and tells her about the institution Mahan established for children with disabilities and special needs. "If you come to Saary, ask for the Ehsan Institution; anyone can give you directions. It's actually Mahan's parents' house."

Nadereh puts the photo on her bookshelf next to Goodarz's and Ehsan's, and places the letter on the table so that eventually she can reply. As the days and weeks pass, though, she can't quite bring herself to write back and Parvaneh's letter remains unanswered.

ACKNOWLEDGEMENTS

My special thanks to Marguerite Anderson and Annie Coyle Martin, two great writers who spent time reading this novel and encouraged me to continue.

Thanks to Gity Nasehi and Sussan Niazi for their constructive comments, dedication, and expertise in helping me with the final translating and editing of the manuscript. I'm also indebted to Constance Dilley, for her edits and her great points of view.

Thank you to Mrs. Ordoobadi, Mohsen Yalfani, Siavoush Daghighian, Nasrin Mohases, Nargess Soudagar, Shiva Maleki, Ava Homa, and Selora Lezerjani who also read my manuscript and whose comments have enriched my manuscript.

My great and utmost acknowledgement goes to Lynn Conningham for her dedication and her skillful editing of this book.

Finally I don't have enough words to thank Luciana Ricciutelli, the Editor-in-Chief of Inanna Publications who accepted my manuscript. I am grateful for her expertise in editing the final version of this book and for her keen knowledge of literature. I'm really thankful to you, Luciana.

I'm also thankful to Renée Knapp, Inanna's fantastic Publicist and Marketing Manager.

I started to write this novel in 2003 but after reading "*We Lived To Tell,* a memoir of Evin prison written by Azadeh Agah, Susan Mehr, and Shadi Parsi (2007), the manuscript went through many changes. I was deeply inspired by the book, and I would like to give the authors of that book a special acknowledgement.

I'm also in debt to M. Raha, the writer of *The Simple Truth,* a memoir in three volumes about the Evin prison.

Photo: Syroos Mohsenzadeh

Mehri Yalfani was born in Hamadan, Iran. She graduated from the University of Tehran with a degree in electrical engineering and worked as an engineer for twenty years. She immigrated to Canada in 1987 with her family, and has been writing and publishing ever since. Four novels and two collections of short stories written in Farsi, her mother tongue, were published in Sweden, the U.S., and Canada. Her novel, *Dancing in a Broken Mirror*, published in Iran, was a finalist for the "Book of the Year" in 2000. She has published several books in English, including *Parastoo: Stories and Poems* (1995), *Two Sisters* (2000), and *Afsaneh's Moon* (2002). Her short fiction has appeared in a number of American and Canadian anthologies. Her most recent collection of short fiction, *The Street of Butterflies,* was published in 2017. She lives and writes in Toronto.